MW01245406

Praise

*P*raise for Donna Alward's Nothing Like a Cowboy

"Donna Alward is one of my go to authors for heartwarming stories and cowboys." – Fresh Fiction

"Alward's novella is perfect for the reader that loves a sweet, "timeless" romance." – Heroes and Heartbreakers

Seducing the Sheriff Copyright
© 2016 by Donna Alward

Nothing Like a Cowboy
Copyright © 2016 by Donna Alward

This book is a work
of fiction. Names, characters, places, and incidents either are products of the
author's imagination or are used fictitiously and are not to be interpreted as
real. Any resemblance to actual persons, living or dead, events, organizations
or locales is entirely coincidental.

All rights reserved.
No part of this book may be reproduced in any form or by any electronic or
mechanical means including information storage and retrieval systems, without
permission in writing from the author. The only exception is by a reviewer, who
may quote brief excerpts in a review.

SEDUCING THE SHERIFF

Donna Alward

Contents

Chapter One   1

Chapter Two   9

Chapter Three   16

Chapter Four   26

Chapter Five   36

Chapter Six   47

Chapter Seven   64

Chapter Eight   77

Chapter Nine   85

Chapter Ten   92

Chapter Eleven   99

Chapter Twelve   111

Nothing Like A Cowboy   117

Chapter One   118

Chapter Two   124

Chapter Three   137

Chapter Four   146

Chapter Five   163

Chapter Six   174

Chapter Seven   183

Chapter Eight   191

Chapter Nine   195

Links   200

About The Author   201

Chapter One

Dinner at The Forge was the best that Joe Lawson could offer a date in the small town of Foundry, Colorado. He straightened his tie, rubbed the toe of his boot against the back of his jeans, let out a massive breath, and then opened the door to the restaurant.

Tracy had set him up on another blind date. He'd tried to get out of it, but his sister knew how to be a real thorn in his side. The woman's name was Janique and she was new in Tracy's office. He scanned the seating area, looking for a woman who matched Tracy's description: early thirties, blond hair, blue eyes, nice figure. Of course, it helped that he knew just about everyone. It didn't take long for him to spot his date—or to realize that she was looking at her watch rather impatiently.

His nerves doubled. He was sheriff in this town. He shouldn't be afraid of a single, harmless female. But he was.

He made his way over to the table, ran a hand over his hair, and put on a smile. "Janique?"

She looked up, her blue eyes assessing before a small smile flirted with her lips, as if he'd somehow passed a first test. "Yes. You're Joe?"

He nodded. "I am. It's nice to meet you. Sorry if I'm a bit late."

She glanced at her watch. "Twenty minutes late, actually."

Heat crept up his neck. "I got hung up at the station. Occupational hazard." He tried another smile. "May I sit?"

"Of course." She leaned back in her chair, the relaxed pose helping to ease his nervousness only a little.

A waitress appeared at his side. "Hello, Joe. Can I get you something to drink?"

He looked up. Cassidy Strong owned The Forge, and as far as he knew, she was able to take on any job in the place, including cook. "Hello, Cassidy. I'll just have water, please."

"Sure thing. Another club soda for you, miss?"

Janique looked up and raised an eyebrow. "It's tonic water. And yes, please. With a fresh slice of lime." She emphasized the "fresh."

Cassidy's eyes sparked for just a moment and he wanted to smile. In his experience, Cassidy was friendly to a fault. He was glad to see she had a little fire left in her. The last time he'd seen her, it was because she'd called the department when her ex, Darren, refused to leave her apartment. When Joe and his deputy arrived, he'd been shocked to see Cassidy so...beaten. If not physically, emotionally. Her body language had made it perfectly clear she was in self-protection mode; her shoulders had been hunched and she'd made herself look smaller, submissive. It hadn't matched his usual impression of her, which was of an attractive, strong, confident woman.

It was also clear that Darren hadn't expected she'd call the police. Surprise had been written all over his face when Joe and Tim stepped to the threshold. Then Darren had turned aggressive and started mouthing off. The resulting names hurled in Cassidy's direction had been enough to put Joe's back up. Escorting Darren off the property had been more of a pleasure than it should have been, professionally speaking.

He'd had a bit of a soft spot for Cassidy ever since.

"Of course," Cassidy said pleasantly, ignoring Janique's snide tone. "I'll be right back with menus."

When she was gone, Janique sighed. "Ugh. I know this is supposed to be the nicest place in town, but the service here leaves something to be desired."

Joe raised an eyebrow. The place was nearly full to capacity; it was a Friday night, after all, and payday. Other than Cassidy, only two waitresses hustled about and one teenage boy bussed tables. "They seem fairly busy. The food will make up for it. Why don't you tell me about yourself?"

She launched into a monologue about her work, her failed marriage, the fact that she had a six year-old son, and a litany of life complaints that had Joe tuning out after about a minute and a half. Cassidy delivered their drinks and menus; he thanked her, but Janique barely even paused for a breath. She certainly didn't bother to say thank you. How on earth had his sister ever thought that they'd be a good match? They had absolutely nothing in common. And while he'd politely inquired about her, she hadn't asked a single question about him.

Janique finally stopped talking and scanned the menu. "Wow. Three whole vegetarian options. A Portobello burger, pasta and marinara, and salad. Predictable." She closed the menu and made a sound of disgust.

Date from hell number...a zillion. At least that's what tonight felt like. His sister, Tracy, was definitely a girly girl when it came to some things—she liked her manis and pedis and a good wine and so on, but she wasn't the least bit demanding. Janique screamed high maintenance. She pulled out her phone and started tapping the screen with long, red fingernails.

He decided he'd order a steak.

Cassidy came back, ready with a smile to take their order. "Are you ready to order?"

Janique sighed. "I suppose I'll have the pasta with marinara. Do you have gluten-free pasta?""Of course."

"I'd like a salad to start, as well. House dressing is fine, but on the side, please."

"Very good. And for you, Joe?"

"The T-bone, medium. Load the baked potato, and whatever the vegetable of the day is, I'll have that."

She smiled a little. "Got it. Can I get you anything else? More to drink?"

Janique shook her head.

"No, thanks, Cass. I think we're fine."

She left again. Silence overcame the table.

They managed to make stilted small talk until their meals arrived. First came the salad, which looked delicious and fresh to Joe's eyes, but apparently lacked flavor in the dressing. He ordered a beer.

When their mains were placed before them, she seemed at least a little satisfied, but glanced over at his steak with derision. He cut into it with more pleasure than he should have felt. If he had to sit through this dinner, and foot the bill besides, he was damned well going to get a meal he enjoyed.

Then her phone rang.

"Excuse me. It's my babysitter."

She answered the phone and he couldn't help overhearing the conversation. "Oh yes, put him on. Yes, honey. Mommy can come home if you don't feel well. Are you sure? I'll leave right now."

Joe put down his fork and steak knife as she hung up.

"I'm sorry, Joe. My little guy isn't feeling well. I'm going to have to cut this short."

Her excuse sounded a little too convenient, but he really wasn't that disappointed. "That's okay. Kids come first."

"He's just been sniffly, but his cough is getting worse. Kids just like to be cuddled when they're sick." She smiled again, then reached for the back of her chair for her coat. As she did so, she put the phone down on the table.

The screen lit up while she was turned around, tugging on the wool jacket. Joe caught a quick glimpse of an incoming text.

You're welcome for the exit strategy. G xx

He leaned back in his chair, disgusted. That was it. No more being set up on dates by his sister. This was the last one.

She pulled on her coat and picked up her phone, dropping it into her pocket as she stood. "It was nice to meet you, Joe. Sorry about this."

"Don't worry about it. I understand completely."

She left so quickly, she almost created a wind tunnel in her wake.

Well. Joe rolled his shoulders and let out a sigh of relief. That torture was over. But it was also kind of awkward, sitting in a restaurant with an empty chair and barely-touched meal across from him.

He dug into his steak. What the hell.

Cassidy came back to the table. "Wow. What happened? Did your date leave?"

He chuckled down low. "Yeah, I got ditched. Of all the blind dates I've had, that might have been the fastest exit."

"She was a blind date."

"Thanks to Tracy."

Cassidy laughed. "Oh. Well. She did seem a little...hard to please."

"Come on now. She just wanted a fresh slice of lime and dressing on the side and you don't have enough vegetarian options, by the way."

Cassidy frowned. "Hmm. That might be something to remember."

He shrugged. "The steak's top notch, though. No complaints from me." He looked up at Cassidy. She wore black pants and a black, button-down shirt, with a little black apron at her waist. Her dark hair was pulled up in some sort of weird twisty knot, and her brown eyes sparkled at him. She was a pretty little thing. He'd never really noticed that before, but since her divorce it seemed she smiled more. She... glowed.

Damn. Glowed? He must be getting soft.

"Hey, Cassidy? When women go on dates, do they have an exit strategy? A way to get out of it or something?"

A blush crept up her cheeks. "Um...well... Yeah, I guess. Sometimes people will have a friend go to the same place and they'll have a sign, you know? Like on a dating site, when you're meeting someone new. A wingman."

"Oh."

"If Tracy set you up...what happened? How come she bolted?"

"She got a phone call. From her kid, apparently. But when she was getting ready to go, she got a text that said 'you're welcome for the exit strategy.'" He frowned. This was all so complicated. Whatever happened to the days when you met someone, planned to go out, and just got on with it?

Cassidy laughed. "Did she have her phone out earlier?"

"Come to think of it, yeah. Just before we ordered."

She looked around, then slid into the vacant chair. "She probably texted someone, told them to call her to give her an out. Sorry, Joe. For what it's worth, I wouldn't ditch you on a date."

Her eyes sparkled at him again. The teasing was just what he needed. "I'm not sure I'm dating material," he answered. "But maybe now Tracy will let up." He spread his hands wide. "I'm a hopeless case."

Cassidy shrugged. "Eh. You're better off. She seemed a little too uptight for you anyway. A little too city."

"You're right."

"Now I'll let you finish your steak before it gets cold." She got up and then nodded at the barely-touched pasta. "You want me to take that away for you?"

"Yeah. I'm not going to eat it." He immediately regretted how it sounded, so he amended, "I mean, not that it's not good. It's just..."

"Relax. It's all good, Joe."

"You could stay, if you like. Keep me company." Did he really just say that? Wouldn't that be hilarious? Start dinner with one woman and finish it with another.

And damned if she didn't look tempted. "Sorry. I'm busier than a one-armed paper hanger tonight, and we're short-staffed. But thanks." A crooked smile touched her lips.

She slipped away, taking the bowl of pasta and the half-eaten salad with her.

It didn't take long for him to finish his meal; with no one to talk to, and a very real awareness that he was sitting alone in the middle of the restaurant, he didn't really feel like lingering. Cassidy came back carrying a plastic container.

"I've brought the bill...and some dessert for you to take with you."

"You didn't have to do that."

She put it down on the table, and slipped the bill beside it. "Hey. Consider it my way of saying sorry you had such a crappy date. I mean, if that had happened to me, I'd have probably been face-first into a tub of ice cream by now."

He laughed. "Thanks." He handed over his credit card, and she took the machine from her apron and processed his payment right at the table. He studied her while her head was bent and her gaze was fixed on the keypad. Why was she still single? She and Darren had been divorced for a while. She was pretty, hardworking, friendly. Beautiful. He couldn't deny that, either. Maybe she was still gun shy about the whole thing. Her ex had been a real jerk.

He might consider asking her out himself, except she scared him a little bit. He'd seen her that afternoon when they'd answered the call at her place. Who knew what had really gone on during their marriage, if it was that acrimonious after it ended? The accepted story was that her ex had cheated and left her when she found out, but Joe knew very well that what was common knowledge was usually just the tip of the iceberg. His gut clenched at the thought of her being hurt in any way. That kind of relationship had to leave a woman with some significant baggage to overcome. She deserved someone who would treat her with kindness. Be gentle and patient.

"Have a good night, Joe." She put her hand on his shoulder briefly. "You too, Cassidy."

He got up and put his wallet back in his pocket, then picked up the take-out dish and left.

It wasn't until he got home, half an hour later, that he opened the dish and saw the note, speared with a toothpick and stuck into a giant piece of cheesecake.

Sorry for the bad date. Dessert is on the house. If you ever want to try my marinara, hit me up.

He got a fork and dug in while thinking about her note. Hit me up? What did that mean? Was it meant to be casual and funny, or was it a subtle invitation?

The chocolate melted on his tongue, rich and sweet. Still, it wasn't the dessert that was the sweetest part of the evening. He couldn't stop thinking about Cassidy's little lopsided smile and the momentary longing in her eyes as she'd turned down his offer to join him. Maybe he'd overlooked something...someone...who'd been right in front of him the whole time.

Chapter Two

Cassidy pulled into the parking lot of the bank at ten minutes to five, ready to put in the day's deposit. She always left it until the last minute on Friday, and then waited until Monday morning to do up the weekend deposit. But it was even later than usual today, because she'd been busy covering a lot of tables while Jenny was out with a bad flu bug.

Bank business was brisk, with a half-dozen customers ahead of her. She took a breath and stood in line, thankful she'd arrived before close. Right now she was looking forward to leaving the restaurant in the capable hands of her manager and heading home for a glass of wine, the dish of pasta carbonara waiting in her car, and a quiet evening.

Then again, all her evenings were quiet these days. The most excitement she'd had was last week when Joe Lawson had his blind date go wrong. She bit down on her lip. There was no denying that Joe was attractive. Hell, not just attractive, but sex-on-a-stick gorgeous.

But she was pretty sure he'd never be interested in her, despite his polite invitation for her to join him the other night. For God's sake, he'd seen her at one of her absolute worst moments. Dealing with the drama between her and her stupid ex would be enough to make a man run in the other direction for good.

Two minutes to five. Any moment now, someone would lock the doors and the people already inside would be served. Anyone else would be out of luck.

Someone came out of an office and walked toward the doors, just as one last person scurried in. The door locks clicked into place.

The line moved forward.

When Cassidy was finally called forward, she had the odd feeling that someone was behind her. She stepped up to the teller with her deposit bag and jumped as she felt something cold and hard against the base of her neck.

"Hello, Cassidy. Here to make your deposit?" the teller asked, still looking at her monitor. When she looked up, her friendly expression turned to one of alarm. "Oh..."

Cassidy's whole body shook as she suddenly realized what was pressing against the hollow at the base of her head.

"Empty your drawers and put all the money into a bag."

The bank had gone deathly quiet.

"I said—" The man raised his voice and reached around Cassidy, pulling her close into his shoulder, while the gun slid to the side of her neck. "Empty your cash drawers right now and put the money into a bag."

Cassidy's heart pounded so hard she could hear it in her ears. The staff at the Foundry First Bank was, like her, frozen in place, struck by fear. Robberies didn't happen here. Foundry was a nice, quiet, small town.

Except apparently things like that did happen. And they were happening *right now*.

Cassidy forced herself to breathe. In, out. In, out. She wouldn't faint. She looked over at her captor, but he had his hoodie pulled all the way up over his head so that it shadowed his face. "Do what he says," she whispered to the teller. "Please."

"I need to use my keys to open the cash drawer," her teller said, her voice shaking.

"Then open it," the man ordered, shaking the gun a little, enough that Cassidy could see it from the corner of her eye. She wished he'd stop pointing it at her. Sometimes those things went off by mistake. Firearm accidents happened all the time. All it would take was him getting agitated and...

Stop. She had to keep her shit together. She dragged her gaze away from the gun.

Her teller's name was Sue, and as far as Cassidy knew, she'd only been working at the bank for a few months. Sue grabbed her keys, and Cassidy saw that her hands were shaking horribly. She struggled to put the key into the lock and dropped the keyring. It made a jingling sound in the heavy silence.

"Hurry up!" His deep voice was impatient, and Sue made a point of apologizing.

"I'm sorry. I'm just nervous. There, see? I've got it."

She opened the drawer. Once he saw her drawer was open, he took a few steps to the left, dragging Cassidy with him. "You," he ordered, waving the gun at another teller. "Open your drawer. Hurry the hell up."

Cassidy didn't struggle. What was the point? He'd take his money, then let her go, wouldn't he? Cold fear shot through her body. She'd do anything to *not* go with him.

The cold metal of the gun touched her neck again and she closed her eyes.

"I said hurry up!"

Staff hurriedly shoved cash into a cloth bag and held it out over the counter. The two other remaining customers had fled to a corner and huddled there, close together, their faces white. "Here," the teller said, her voice shaking. "Take it."

"Put it on the counter and back away."

He loosened his grip just a bit, holding onto Cassidy's arm instead of her whole body, as he reached for the bag with his gun hand. When he turned back, she got a good look at his face. He'd deliberately kept his head down, but when he reached for the money and then turned, the hood on his jacket pulled back just a bit and she met his gaze.

She knew him.

Her body went numb. She didn't know his name, but the face was somehow familiar. The hazel eyes, long jaw, straight nose, and rather full lips. She'd seen him somewhere before...but where? She looked away quickly, hoping he hadn't glimpsed recognition on her face. He resumed his earlier posture of pulling her in against his shoulder, but he didn't put the gun against her head this time. Instead, he pulled her with him toward the exit, ordered someone to unlock the door, and just as he stepped through, he ripped the deposit bag from her hand and gave her a rough shove, sending her directly into the bank employee.

He disappeared out the door.

For several seconds there was stunned silence. Then bedlam erupted.

A couple of the tellers started crying. The customers got up from their crouched posture and went for the seating area, pale and shaken. Roberta, the bank manager, unlocked her office and came out. "Is everyone okay?" She hustled to the front doors and locked them again. Cassidy looked at the clock on her phone. 5:02. The whole thing had taken place in less than four minutes, but it had felt like forever. Mechanically, she found a chair and sank into it.

She heard sirens now. Roberta was speaking; the banking staff was responding, but none of the words registered. All she heard were the sirens getting closer, and all she could see was the guy's face. She scrambled to place it. Was he from town? No. Foundry was small, and owning a restaurant meant that she knew most people. Had he come from another town or city, then? But where? What was the common thread?

The sirens stopped and Cassidy was dimly aware of Roberta going back to the doors to open them for the police. When she looked up, four uniformed officers entered the bank. Leading the group was Joe Lawson, looking very big and official and...safe. As his gaze touched hers, she let out a long, slow breath. There was something instantly reassuring in his presence. She was okay now. Joe was here.

Something in her brain clicked. She had it. She'd seen the guy's face online. On...a profile.

She grabbed a nearby garbage can and vomited.

Cassidy Stone's face was pale, and Joe saw her sway in her seat as if she was going to faint. Instead, she bent and threw up in a garbage can. He grimaced. People had varying reactions to stress and trauma. It wasn't such a big shock that she'd been sick to her stomach. He'd seen worse.

He went over and squatted down in front of her. "Hey, Cassidy." There was a box of tissues on the glass-topped table next to her, and he plucked one from the box and handed it to her. She wiped her mouth and tossed the tissue in the trash, then deftly tied the bag in a knot.

"Sorry," she gasped. "I couldn't help it."

He laughed a little, hoping he could help her relax. "Hey, you hit the trash can. You did good."

She tucked a strand of hair behind her ear and chuckled, but it sounded weak. "Mind if I put my head between my knees for a second?"

"Take your time." He needed to ask her questions, and the sooner the better, but she was no good to him if she was passed out on the floor. He stood and put his hand on her shoulder, just briefly, but hoped it was reassuring. "You were here during the robbery?"

She nodded, the strand of hair coming loose again. "He...he held a gun to my head." The word was slightly muffled from her odd posture. "I guess I was the leverage."

Shit. An image of her shot into his brain. He imagined her being held hostage like that. She wouldn't have crumpled. She would have stayed calm. Terrified, but calm. Her calmness had probably kept things from escalating. It hurt his heart to think that she might have learned that from personal experience.

"Are you hurt?"

She shook her head and sat up again. "Just shaken. Really shaken, apparently. I never puke."

He couldn't help but chuckle at that. "We're going to make sure you're okay. We'll take statements from everyone. There are cameras everywhere, too. Don't worry."

She nodded and the piece of hair bounced with the movement. He resisted the urge to tuck it back into place. Instead he took his hand off her shoulder and stepped back.

"Boss?" Tim Clark looked over the counter. "I've got a description. I'm gonna send it out now.""Vehicle?"

"No one saw. He might have gone on foot."

"Set up roadblocks on the exits to the highway. We might be too late, but you never know."

"On it."

"Cass?"

She let out a breath. She was still pale, but not that sickly gray-green color she'd been only moments before. The crest of each cheek held a dot of pink. She was going to be fine.

"He's not from here," she said, shaking her head. "Not from town. But I can maybe tell you where."

"Maybe?" Intrigued, he squatted down and leaned closer. "What do you mean?"

"I mean, I recognized him. He had his hood up and tried to hide his face, but when he reached for the bag of money, I saw."

"You got a name?" A fizz of adrenaline ripped through him. This would speed things up a lot. The robber hadn't worn a mask or balaclava, but even with video, it could take a while to get an actual ID.

She shook her head. "No name. But I can find it for you."

The color was back in her cheeks, and her gaze slid away for a moment. "Give me a minute to check something."

She reached for her purse and took out her phone. He waited impatiently, tapping the toe of his boot. The guy had robbed a bank and with every minute that passed, the farther away he got. "Cassidy?" "I've got to scroll through. Maybe I'm wrong..." She huffed out a breath. "Thirty more seconds, I swear."

He could tell when she found what she was looking for, because her eyes widened and her lips turned down in a strange sort of frown. She looked up, met his gaze, and then handed him the phone, screen first.

He took it, warm from her hand, and stared at the screen.

"A dating site?"

"Don't judge, Mr. Blind Date Disaster. Anyway, that's him. That profile. I'm sure of it."

"I'll be right back. Sit tight."

He took her phone with him and rushed to put things in motion.

Chapter Three

C assidy pressed her hands between her knees to keep them from shaking. Her whole body vibrated, and she kept seeing the dark barrel of the gun. It was weird for that one, tiny image to fill her brain. She tried diverting her thoughts to something else. A bobble head on one of the teller counters, resembling a hockey player from the Avalanche. Nope. Cold metal barrel. The sign on top of the counter in red and white that said, "Ask me about our high-interest savings account." Nope. She swallowed and looked around. There was Joe, busy with three other officers, their heads together. She let her gaze travel down his body to where his trousers fit perfectly against a very fine bottom.

That worked for about two seconds, and then the sickening lurch came back and so did the image.

She had to calm the hell down. It was over. She was safe. No more gun against her neck.

Joe came back, a look of concern pulling at his features. "Cassidy," he said gently. "It's okay. You're safe now."

She gave a shaky laugh. "I know. I've been repeating that to myself over and over. I think I just need to give it some more time."

"You're in shock. And there'll be someone to talk to you about that, too. To make sure you don't suffer any long-term effects."

She nodded. He meant some sort of victim counseling. "Seriously, though? I survived my divorce. I'll survive this." She tried to laugh again. "There's nothing more terrifying than dividing marital assets through two lawyers."

She shuddered at the memory. Darren hadn't been an easy husband. He'd made an even worse ex. He'd been the one to leave and he'd asked for everything. The house. The car. Their savings. If Cassidy hadn't needed the money so badly, she would have given him all of it and said good riddance. Instead she'd fought him for her share, and the divorce had gotten ugly.

"At least you didn't have a custody battle, too," Joe offered kindly.

She winced. Yes, no kids had been caught in the middle. But that wasn't because she hadn't wanted them. She had. She'd kept the car, he'd bought out his half of the house and lived there now with his girlfriend, and the savings had been split in half. She'd saved herself a good amount of stress and lawyer fees by taking that much and not asking for any alimony.

There was something to be said for being free and clear. And when the evenings and weekends were a little too quiet, she reminded herself that loneliness was better than the alternative—living with a liar and a cheat.

Joe crouched down in front of her. "I'm going to have Sam—Deputy White—take you to the station while we check this out. You'll be safe there and we can update you soon, but we'll also have more questions and take an official statement."

She frowned. "I have to go sit at the station? Really?"

"Sorry. It's just...well. The thing is, Cass, if you recognized him, then he might have recognized you. We don't want to take any chances."

A woozy hum echoed in her ears. Joe was right. What if he knew who she was and that she could identify him?

"This is bad. This is really bad."

Joe smiled. "It'll be okay. We just want to take precautions. Having his identity is huge. We'll catch him, I promise." He patted her knee.

Cassidy wasn't quite sure what to think. So many emotions pressed down on her right now that she felt both hypersensitive and oddly numb.

"Cass, go with Sam. He'll look after you."

Right or wrong, she grabbed onto the only lifeline she knew. "You'll come back?"

"I'll come back." He smiled at her, and she looked into his gray-green eyes. They were warm and serious and...honest. And just about the only thing she could hold on to at this moment.

"Okay."

"Oh, and Cass?"

"Hmm?""Not My 1st Rodeo? Really?"

Damn, the heat rushed back to her cheeks again. "I said don't judge. Isn't everyone on a dating site these days?"

"Not everyone. Some of us have had our fill of blind dates," he responded, and then winked at her.

The bit of humor was welcome, made the situation feel a tiny bit more normal. "What, throwing in the towel?"

He chuckled, then touched her knee again. "Make sure you get some food and water and take time to breathe. It'll feel more normal again soon."

"Easy for you to say," she muttered.

Joe left, taking one of the other deputies with him. Sam came over, looking horribly official for his what, twenty-three years? He was probably still wet behind the ears. But he nodded at her politely and said, not unkindly, "Are you ready to go, Ms. Strong?"

"As ready as I'll ever be." She stood up and willed her knees not to shake.

All she'd wanted was a quiet Friday night with Netflix and a bottle of wine and some comfort food. Sure, there were times when she'd imagined what it would be like if her life weren't so boring or predictable, but this was overkill as far as adventure-seeking went.

She followed Sam out of the bank and into the waiting squad car.

It was over an hour before Joe came back to the small police station. Sam had let her wait in one of the offices, which was more comfortable than the utilitarian interrogation rooms. Of which there were two, and one appeared to be full of boxes.

He poked his head into the room. "You doing okay?"

She nodded, and sat forward in her chair. "Did you get him?" she asked, hoping that the whole ordeal was over and the guy was in custody.

He frowned. "No, not yet. Did Sam take your statement?"

"He did." That had been humiliating. She'd had to explain to the deputy about the dating site. Not that he'd asked any personal questions. But she'd had to log in and find the profile again. Jonathan Graves, the name said. A bull-rider from Greeley.

Joe came inside the office and pulled a chair up to the desk. It creaked as he sat in it, and she realized how long his legs were when he stretched them out, crossing his ankles. "The roadblocks will be up for a while yet, but I'm guessing he's out of the area. He won't get far, though. ID-ing him so quickly means we'll be able to get a plate number for whatever he's driving."

"Good, good," she murmured. The whole thing felt surreal and put her off-balance. The fear and shock had abated some, though. She reached for the nearly cool cup of tea the receptionist had brought her several minutes ago.

"Hey, boss?"

Joe looked up at Sam, standing in the doorway to the office. "Yeah? Any developments?"Sam shook his head. "Actually, a snag. Turns out

Jonathan Graves isn't his real name. He's using an alias on the site."

Cassidy put her forehead on her hand. "This is why I don't do dating sites. No one is who they say they are."

Joe chuckled and put his hand on her shoulder. "First time, huh?"

She looked up, more miserable than before. "First and last." Maybe this was something they'd laugh about later. Him with his disappearing date and her with her online dating disaster. They could commiserate over their sad excuses for love lives.

"Can you stick around a bit longer?" he asked.

She saw something in his expression that sent warning bells through her head. He was trying to stay relaxed and downplay the situation, wasn't he? The other employees and witnesses had given their statements, been given contact information for counseling services, and gone home with family. But not her. They kept asking her to stay behind.

"I guess. Though I'd like to go home."

Home. To an empty house. There was zero chance she was going to sleep tonight.

"I promise it won't be much longer." He turned to Sam. "I'll be right out. We'll get a warrant to access this guy's information from the internet provider."

He squeezed her shoulder and then stood. "Hang tight, okay?"

"Do I have a choice?" Irritation mingled with exhaustion now. She was quite worn out from the rollercoaster of adrenaline and emotion today.

"No," he admitted.

Not longer turned out to be a couple of hours, which dragged on interminably. Cassidy browsed on her phone for a while, but the battery was getting low, so she shut it off and tucked it into her purse. She tried to relax enough to nod off, but when she closed her eyes she saw the robbery play out again in her mind. Around seven, a clerk she didn't recognize brought in a paper bag with take-out—pepperoni pizza, a small salad, and soda. This wasn't what she'd planned for a relaxed Friday night. She was still in her work clothes and sitting at the police station, instead of comfy in fuzzy pajamas and curled up on the sofa watching Netflix. Cooling pizza and a room-temperature soda instead of wine and pasta. Tiny details, she thought, regaining a little of her sense of humor as she thanked the clerk for the food.

That she managed to actually eat was a good sign, she figured. Earlier, the thought of food had made her stomach turn.

It was almost eight o'clock when Joe came into the office again. "Sorry for the wait, Cassidy," he said, dropping a folder on the desk. "It took longer than we expected."

"Did you get him?"

He frowned. "No. Not yet. We got his real name, though. And information's coming in. He can't hide forever." He lifted his chin and sniffed the air. "Sheri got you something to eat, unless my nose deceives me. Pizza?"

She patted her belly. "Yes. Thank you. I actually ate!" She smiled up at him. "Considering, you know. *Lunch.*" She gave a shudder. Lunch was now somewhere in the dumpster behind the bank.

He laughed. "You sound better now. I was worried about you for a while. You were really white."

"I was really scared." She let the smile slip off her face as she looked up at Joe. He was imposing in his uniform, but in a reassuring way. His hair was so dark it was nearly black, and his serious eyes lent his appearance a sort of gravity that made him seem responsible and... reliable. A protector. She licked her lips and asked the simple question that had been on her mind for the last two hours. "Do you really think I might be in danger, Joe? That he recognized me?"

"Is it likely? Maybe not. But I'd rather not take any chances. This guy was desperate enough to have a gun. Not just that, but he held it against you and took you hostage. Until we know more, I'd like to make sure you're safe."

Unease swirled in her stomach. "What does that mean, exactly?"

"It means that tonight you'll have protection at your house."

The thought of having cops in her tiny apartment made her feel ill all over again. Right after the divorce, Darren had forced his way into her new place, accusing her of all sorts of crazy stuff. She'd had to call the cops then, and Joe had been one of the officers who'd answered the call. She wasn't going to mention that, though. It was too humiliating and she would rather leave the incident behind her.

"Isn't there another option? I'm in a building with other tenants. I would hate to make them feel uneasy, too."

He sat down in one of the guest chairs. It was odd that their positions were reversed: her behind the desk in the big rolling chair, and him in the vinyl chair reserved for visitors.

"The only accommodation in town is the bed and breakfast, and that has its own challenges. We'd have to go up the interstate to a motel—"

"And there would be extra charges involved with that." She cut him off before he could state the obvious.

"I can't deny that budgets are tight around here."

"I'll do what you think is best, Joe." She looked up at him and held his gaze. "I trust you."

Their gazes held for several seconds, and something different caught in her chest, shortening her breaths. He looked like he actually cared. About her. Not just as a witness, but as a person. Maybe it was because Foundry was a small town and people looked after each other. Maybe because anytime they met around town, they always managed to make small talk, including last week when his date had bailed on him. But this felt like more. She just hoped it wasn't pity. Either for this afternoon or for all the horrible things Darren had spewed out of his mouth the day he'd refused to leave her apartment. Most of all, she hoped he didn't believe any of it. Darren had made her sound like the most manipulative woman on the planet. Nine times out of ten, she put those horrible words in perspective and shrugged them off. But now and again, when she was feeling vulnerable, they came back to haunt her. Today was a double whammy; she'd been involved in a crime scene and she was sitting across from Sheriff Lawson, who was attractive enough—and nice enough—to make any woman nervous.

"There is one other option, though I don't think you'll like it."

"Oh?" His words dragged her out of her thoughts. "You could stay with me. I'm supposed to be off duty this weekend anyway. It wouldn't pull anyone off the investigation, and it's budget-friendly. Plus, I guarantee the bed is more comfortable than the ones at the roadside motel." He raised an eyebrow.

She sat back in the chair. Stay with Joe? "So you mean you'd be my protection detail?"

He chuckled. "That's very official sounding of you. But yeah, essentially. If you don't mind peace and quiet, that is. My cabin's pretty remote."

She frowned, pulling her brows together. "How remote?"

"I've got a little place up Siskin Mountain."

Siskin Mountain...the road only went in a few miles and then it was all dirt tracks leading to hunting lodges and the like. She'd gone hiking in the area a few times and found it beautiful. "Do you have electricity?"

He laughed. "Yes, of course. I'm not that far in, Cass. Power and running water and a generator back-up. Unless someone knows exactly where they're going, though, they'll drive right by the lane. You could look at it as a weekend getaway. Bring a few books. A couple of DVDs. I don't have internet up there, so if you want to go online you'll have to use your data on your phone. I do get cell coverage. Most of the time, anyway." He grinned. "And I have a land line."

She thought about it. It did sound much more preferable to being cooped up in her apartment with cops outside her door or sleeping on her sofa. And truth be told, the idea of a few days surrounded by peace and quiet, by trees and birds and wildlife...sounded lovely. Just because the situation was unusual didn't mean she should suffer for it.

There was just one problem. It was Joe's place. And Joe would be there. And that was a bit weird. And intimate. She'd known him a long time, but only in, well, passing. Not exactly *this* level of friendship. She bit her lip. If he could have read her mind a few minutes ago, he'd be retracting his invitation fast enough.

"You probably don't want some stranger taking over your place," she replied, folding her hands in her lap. "It's a sweet offer, Joe, but I don't want to impose."

"You wouldn't be, and you're hardly a stranger. I can keep an eye on you, and if I have to come into town, I know you'll be okay there. Besides, it'll probably only be for a night. At some point this guy will use a credit card or his bank account, or he'll contact someone, and we'll have him."

Him. "You said you identified him?"

"Chad. Chad Winters. He put a fake name on his profile, but it wasn't too hard to follow the trail from the site to his IP address."

One night. She could handle that. Besides, if there were cops outside her building, Darren would go ballistic. Even though they were divorced and he had no claim on her, he inserted himself in her business again and again, usually to criticize something. It was amazing to her that he still thought he had a say in anything she did.

"I'll have to stop by my place and grab a few things. Some clothes and a toothbrush and stuff."

"We can do that."

"You're sure it's not overkill? I could go home and be fine."He hesitated for a long moment. "I'd rather be safe than sorry. And I wouldn't want you to stay alone tonight, anyway. I doubt you're finished with being shaken up over the whole thing."

That thought had crossed her mind. She had to admit that the idea of having someone nearby was comforting. "What time do you want to go?"

"In a half hour or so? I'm going to finish up here and then we'll make a quick stop in at your apartment."

"Okay."

He put his hands on his knees and stood. "I'll be back as soon as I can," he said, and giving a quick nod, left her alone in the office yet again.

She could do this and be fine. Besides, Joe had no idea she found him the least bit attractive. She'd just have to make sure it stayed that way.

Chapter Four

The paved road had ended several hundred yards past, and Cassidy bounced as the bumps of the dirt road vibrated through Joe's rugged SUV. He slowed, though Cassidy couldn't see anything in the inky darkness. The beams of his headlights lit a small swath straight ahead, showing the gravel in front of them and the hulking shapes of the trees. Joe turned into a narrow lane and she held her breath. She didn't mind the forest; it had to be the unfamiliar area and the darkness causing the anxious feeling of claustrophobia.

"Okay?" Joe asked. He hadn't spoken for a long time, though Cassidy hadn't minded the silence. It'd been comfortable, peaceful.

"Feeling a little out of my depth," she admitted. "How do you know where you are? It's so dark out here."

He grinned; she watched as his face relaxed into the expression, lit by the bluish glow of the dashboard lights. "Habit, I guess. After a while, trees are familiar. Their height, the way they're grouped...plus I've driven this so many times now it's just second nature."

Another ten seconds and Cassidy saw a faint glow through the trees. "We're close?"

"We're here." He pulled into a clearing and parked the truck next to a small cabin. Cassidy couldn't see much in the darkness, and the outside light only illuminated a small circle around the door.

She undid her seatbelt and hopped out of the truck. Joe had already grabbed her bag and was leading the way to the cabin. Once inside, he flicked on some lights so that the windows glowed in welcome. Cassidy squared her shoulders and followed him. She might as well make the best of it. And there was something to be said for peace and quiet.

It was cold inside the cabin. September meant that the evenings cooled off significantly, particularly in the mountains. She rubbed her arms, trying to get warm. Joe, still wearing his jacket, was already at the wood stove, stacking kindling and newspaper. He lit a match and touched the paper. Little flicks of flame devoured the newsprint and caught at the thin kindling.

"Sorry about the cold. Nice thing about a small space is that it won't take long to heat up."

"I love a fire. Don't worry about it."

She looked around. The outside of the cabin hadn't deceived at all. It was small, but undeniably cozy. He'd turned on a lamp on a side table, and she saw that the furniture was simple and sturdy, a masculine brown corduroy with a fleece blanket thrown over the back of the overstuffed chair. There was a television and DVD player on a wood stand. No cable box. Between that and no internet, she could forget about streaming any series or movies. Good thing he'd suggested bringing along some DVDs. She swallowed against a lump in her throat. What a sad statement of her life, that a weekend with a hunky guy at a remote cabin meant making sure she had enough DVDs and books to get her through.

The fire crackled merrily and Joe stood, stretching out his back. She took a good look at him. He'd shed his puffy jacket and loosened his tie, unbuttoning the top button of his shirt so that a tiny V of skin peeked out.

And she was here with him. Alone. In his cabin in the woods with not another soul around for what could be miles.

"It should be warm in a few minutes. Can I get you something? Tea? I think I have some around here somewhere. Just the plain bags from the grocery store. Or instant coffee?" He looked a little sheepish. "It's kind of a bachelor's place. There's not much that's fancy about it."

"Stop apologizing." She smiled at him. "Actually, I love it. I'm a country girl at heart. Granted, instant coffee isn't usually my speed, but this isn't even close to roughing it, Joe. Thanks for putting up with me."

He rubbed his hands together. "Are you hungry? I do have food. And I know how to cook."

"I had pizza."

"Right."

She suddenly realized that she hadn't seen him eat. "Wait. You didn't, did you? Have dinner, I mean."

"There wasn't much time."

"I'm not really hungry, but if you want to have dinner, I'll sit with you, maybe have a drink of something. Unless you'd rather be alone."

Joe reached for a couple of pieces of wood and tossed them on the snapping kindling. "This is kind of awkward, isn't it?"

She nodded. "To be honest, we know each other, but we're not really friends. Oh, that sounded horrible. That's not what I meant..." Way to go, Cass, she chided herself. She sounded like a total nitwit.

He came forward and put his hands on her upper arms. "We're not friends *yet*. Why don't we say that? And I'd like it if you hung out with me while I have something to eat. It's kind of nice having someone around." He grinned crookedly. "Hey, it'll be the second time in a week that you'll be keeping me company while I have a meal solo."

She laughed. "Okay, then. Since you put it that way. I even promise I won't ditch you."

"Let me take your bag and put it in the bedroom."

She bit down on her lip. The bedroom? There was only one? He was giving her his bed, wasn't he? There was a certain intimacy, thinking about sleeping in the sheets where he normally slept. In his room. On his mattress. She hoped she wasn't blushing as she looked up at him. "Joe, that's not necessary. I can take the couch. I don't want to put you out."

"Don't be silly. The couch is fine for me. I've slept in much worse spots." He grinned. "Besides, if we'd gone to your apartment, I would have slept on the couch there, right?"

He took her bag and led the way into the bedroom. "You might want to keep the door open, though, to let the heat in. It's supposed to be cold tonight. Only thirty-eight degrees."

He flicked on the bedroom light. The bed was neatly made, covered with what appeared to be a very old, handmade quilt pieced in burgundy, navy, and brown blocks. A laundry basket sat on a wood chair with folded clothes piled inside. There was a clock radio on a table next to the bed, and a book—some sort of crime thriller by an author she recognized. "You read?"

"Don't sound so surprised. I like to read before I go to sleep."

But she was surprised. Darren had always said reading was pointless, because non-fiction was boring or depressing and fiction was just made up shit that would never happen. He was right about that. She'd often caught herself looking over at him and realizing that there was no dashing fairytale in the works for her. Gallantry was simply not in Darren's vocabulary.

Hell, Joe had shown more gallantry and chivalry in one day than Darren had showed her in five years of marriage. Sometimes it was hard to remember why she'd married him in the first place.

"I really don't want to put you out of your bed," she said, turning to face him. He'd already put her bag on top of a small chest.

"Cassidy, you're sleeping in the bed. The only option left is the sofa. Unless you not wanting to put me out of the bed means that we share it."

She must have looked horrified because he laughed, a rich, full sound. "Oh, my God. You should see your face. I'm joking." He shoved his hands in his pockets. "Maybe I shouldn't joke. You've had a crazy day."

Funny, how standing in his bedroom made her forget a lot of what had happened. But it came rushing back now; the real reason she was standing here. This Chad guy. Who'd waved a gun in her face. Who might know who she was, because she *hadn't* lied on her profile. Maybe she should have been more careful...

"Come on, let's go to the kitchen. I'll make a sandwich and get us a drink and we can relax."

She followed him and accepted a glass of whiskey to steady her nerves as he built a sandwich and threw a handful of potato chips on a plate to go with it. "You want some?" he asked.

"Why the hell not?" she asked. Chips were a weakness of hers, and she was already feeling the effects of the liquor. Joe added another splash to her glass, put a couple of fingers into a glass of his own, and they headed back to the living room to sit on the sofa and chill.

The fire was well-established now and threw a steady heat. Joe left in the grate and kept the wood stove door open so that they could watch the flames dance and flicker, the light from the fire casting shadows on the walls. Cassidy curled her feet up beneath her and cradled her glass in her hand. The bowl of chips rested on her left knee, and she picked up a chip and bit into it, loving salty taste as it melted on her tongue.

"So," Joe asked, swallowing a mouthful of sandwich, "why Not My 1st Rodeo?"

She'd expected they'd get around to talking about the dating site eventually. She regretted ever signing up now, though it had seemed like a good idea at the time.

"I don't know. Foundry is a small town. Trying to meet new people is...well, there's not a lot of selection."

"Ouch."

She chuckled. "Oh, that's just your wounded pride talking. Shut up."

He laughed too, and took another bite as the comfort level in the room increased.

"The thing is, everyone knows about my divorce. They probably know more than I'd like, really, and who wants to take on that kind of baggage? This site is kind of specific. It's for people who've been married before. And, well, it's for those who enjoy a rural lifestyle."

"Farmers."

"And ranchers or what not. I grew up in a rural community. I love wide open space and I miss it. I wasn't sad when we moved here. It's small but it reminds me of home just a little bit. The good and the bad," she said, raising one eyebrow. "I left my family behind, but I saw pictures of the mountains and the ranches in the area and... yeah."

"So you're looking for a rancher."

Was she? Did she really want to be a farm wife? She had to admit she wouldn't mind it, but it was more than that.

She took another sip of whiskey. She'd had enough now that the edges of her restraint had softened somewhat. "Maybe I'm just romanticizing the kind of man I think ranchers are. Hardworking, loyal, ordinary, know-how-to-treat-their-women kind of guys."

"You didn't have that with your husband."

"I thought I did. I was wrong, though."

"I heard he kind of failed on the loyalty front."

"If you mean loyalty to be synonymous with fidelity, you've nailed it."

She took a bigger gulp this time.

"I did, and I'm sorry. That's an asshole move on his part."

"Yes, it is. Anyway, he's gone now. For the most part." She looked up at Joe. "Would you ever cheat on someone, Joe?"

No sooner was it out of her mouth than she regretted it. "Forget I asked that! That was totally out of line. I'm sorry."

He shrugged. "Don't be. And no, I wouldn't. I've always said that a person should get out of a relationship first if they want to be with someone else so badly."

She agreed. It still made her sick to her stomach thinking about her husband being with his now-girlfriend, and then coming home and crawling into bed with her. She'd once used the term "double dipping" with him and it had made him furious. The truth hurt. So had his anger.

Joe put his plate down on the coffee table. "Listen. I know Darren is a jackass. I was working the day you called to have him removed from your apartment, remember? He seems to be having a hard time letting go."

"Which is ironic considering he was the one to have the affair. Anyway, it's in the past."

"And now you're looking at dating again."

She laughed, lifting her glass in salute. "Know what's even better? My profile's only been up on the site for a few weeks. I haven't even had any dates yet. I was kind of getting freaked out about it, wondering what the hell was wrong with me, when today happened."

His somber, gray gaze touched hers. "There's nothing wrong with you."

She laughed again, a little knot of nerves tightening in her belly at his words. She drained her glass. She was definitely feeling a little woozy and less guarded than she probably should be. "Oh, there's plenty wrong. Ask my ex."

"Not really a credible source, I don't think," Joe countered. "Here, let me take that glass."

"Is there any more?"

"I think you're in a good place now, Cass. Wouldn't want to ruin it."

"Right. You've already seen me throw up once today." She smiled at him, too bleary to be appalled. "That was pretty embarrassing."

"Like I said, I've seen worse. And you did hit the garbage can." He put her empty glass on his plate. "It's getting late. Maybe you want to try to get some sleep."

"Maybe. You do have a bathroom, right? I need to brush my teeth. And pee." She looked up at him and shrugged. "I think I lost my verbal filter somewhere. Sorry."

"It's just the adrenaline of the day, combined with fatigue and whiskey. It tends to have that effect. Don't worry about it. I'll show you the bathroom." He grinned at her and stood, holding out his hand. She took it, let him tug her to her feet, and tried not to think about how strong and warm his fingers were around hers.

She brushed her teeth and put on pajamas while tidying sounds came from the kitchen. At least she hadn't grabbed her short nightie. It was bound to get cold in the night and there was some dignity to maintain. She'd packed pink-and-white PJs and she buttoned the shirt all the way to the top button. She left her bra on, too, not wanting to sport the "untethered" look in front of Joe. Well, maybe she did. Which was precisely why she shouldn't. She hadn't lost all sense.

"I'm going to head in," she called out, making a beeline for the bedroom. She scrambled beneath the sheets and pulled the blanket up to her chin. The mattress was comfortable; only a double size, but with plenty of room for one, or two if they wanted to be cozy. She heard Joe adding wood to the fire and then stoking it for the night; she closed her eyes and inhaled, and the scent of him rose up out of the bedding. The intimacy she'd worried about earlier came crashing back, and she pictured him sleeping in the bed, his dark hair on the pillow. She wondered if he slept in a T-shirt or just underwear...she just bet his chest would be muscled with a sprinkling of dark hair. The muscles between her legs tightened and her breasts ached a little. Damn that whiskey. Damn her dry spell. Damn Joe for being so nice and so...sexy.

He knocked on the doorframe. "Cassidy? Sorry, but I need to grab a pillow and a couple of spare blankets. I didn't think you'd be in bed this fast."

His voice was low and husky and sent shivers along her skin.

"It's okay. Go ahead."

He got blankets out of the chest, but the pillow was the one on the other side of the bed. The slight weight of his hands pressed against the bed as he turned down the quilt and slipped the pillow from beneath it. He was leaning over the bed a little and she wanted to reach for his tie and pull him onto the mattress with her.

She could have died today. Now, in the stillness, that fact was seeping back into her consciousness, but without the buffer of adrenaline and shock. She could have died. But Joe was here and he was looking after her. Looking after her when no one else did. Even if it was his job, she appreciated it. More than he'd ever know.

"Good night," he whispered, and she felt the absence of him as he stepped back from the bed.

"Good night, Joe," she whispered back.

The light stayed on in the living room for a little while; the glow of it crept over the doorway of the bedroom. Cassidy knew she shouldn't, but she slid over to the far side of the bed and watched quietly as Joe spread the blankets on the sofa and plumped the pillow at one end. But the best part was when he stripped off his tie and unbuttoned his shirt. She was right. He did have just the slightest bit of chest hair, and his upper body appeared hard and muscled. Her mouth went dry as he reached for the button on his pants, and she saw a flash of gray underwear as he dropped his uniform on the chair and then crawled under the blankets.

No pajamas, then. No T-shirt. Just a pair of briefs and skin. Warm, soft skin.

She waited a long time, listening for the sound of snoring. But her eyes grew heavy, and curled up in warm blankets with Joe's woodsy scent surrounding her, she fell asleep.

Chapter Five

Listening to Cassidy's deep breathing was nearly doing him in.

Joe turned over onto his side, wishing he could fall asleep. Crime in their little town was generally the mild sort, and armed robbery was a total anomaly. But it wasn't the seriousness of the crime keeping him awake. It was Cassidy, in his bed, dressed in some flimsy pink pajamas.

Bringing her here might have been a mistake. In the office, it had seemed perfectly sensible and platonic. They'd always been friendly. But sitting with her on the sofa as she got tipsy on a little bit of whiskey was something else. She brought out his protective instincts. She brought out more than that, too. When she'd looked up at him and said that she trusted him today...something had changed. He'd felt it, like a thump to the chest. There was something about the way she'd looked into his eyes. Nothing was completely platonic. They were two people of roughly the same age, single, and damn, she was pretty. Even during the stress of the day, she'd managed to crack a few jokes. He admired that.

He flipped over to his other side and closed his eyes, focused on slowing his breathing, and tried to lull himself into sleep. If only he could shut off his brain.

She'd asked for more whiskey, and he'd been tempted to give it to her. But he'd also known it would be a mistake to indulge. He was supposed to be looking after her. He definitely wasn't supposed to be staring at her lips and thinking about kissing her. That would be totally inappropriate, considering the circumstances. He'd brought her here out of duty. Nothing more. Except she'd gone from sweet to sexy as hell right before his eyes, and he'd done the responsible thing and cut her off. For both their sakes.

He was nearly asleep when her breathing changed. At first it was barely noticeable; just a hitch as she inhaled, and only every few breaths. But then her breathing sounded jerky and panicked. He sat up a bit, listening closely. Was she having a nightmare? He waited, wondering if she'd calm, not wanting to wake her if he didn't have to.

She made a few incoherent sounds, and what he thought were jumbled words that didn't make any sense. Torn between going into the bedroom or staying put, he tightened his fingers around the cushion of the sofa and held his breath.

And then she screamed.

He was off the sofa in a heartbeat, across the room and into the dark bedroom. Cassidy was still asleep, and when he touched her, her muscles tensed beneath his fingers. "Cassidy, it's Joe. Wake up."

He sat on the bed as she made a strangled sound. Shit. "Cassidy." He spoke a bit louder. "Cassidy, wake up. You're having a bad dream."

She came awake with a huge gasp, and even in the darkness her eyes were wide and scared. Her chest rose and fell rapidly, and he tried to bring her out of the fear and into the present. "It's Joe, Cassidy. You're okay. You're at my place and no one is going to hurt you."

"Joe?" She sat up, and then the trembling started. He ran his hands down the soft fabric of her sleeves. She shook beneath his touch.

"Yes, it's Joe. It's over now. You're okay."

She started to cry. What the hell was he supposed to do about that?

"Here, here," he soothed, and scooched up on the bed, gathering her in his arms as he went. She was shaking all over and gasping with little disjointed sobs. "Shh," he said, feeling utterly helpless.

"H-he was there. His face. But I could only see the g-gun." She shuddered. "When it happened, all I could see was that black barrel. I kept waiting for it to go off."

"But it didn't."

"I...it did in my dream. Oh, God..."

"Hush," he said, pulling her closer. "Hang on to me. I'm not going to let anything happen to you, okay?"

She nodded against his shoulder. "I'm sorry." The apology was drawn out, a pathetic little wail that reached in and touched his heart. She'd been strong all day. Even right after the robbery, she'd had a physical reaction and then had dealt with whatever needed to be done.

He'd hoped the whiskey would help her relax and sleep straight through the night. But the nightmare wasn't that surprising, really. After holding herself together all day, it was in sleep that the truth met no barriers.

"Don't apologize. You don't have anything to be sorry for. Just breathe. Nice, slow breaths. You're okay. You're at my cabin, and I'm here with you, and you're fine."

He moved to sit back a little, but she clutched his arms, keeping him close. "Don't go away yet, okay?"

He swallowed tightly. It was torture, holding her this close, but he wouldn't leave her, either. He rubbed his hand on her shoulder. "I'm right here."

She shifted her weight and his body tightened in response. Dammit. Her pajamas covered most of her body and weren't particularly sexy, but it didn't matter. They were soft and warm, like her. They smelled like vanilla and sugar...or was that her skin? She was nearly on his lap now, and if she moved another few inches it would be potentially embarrassing for them both. He only wore cotton shorts. The air in the bedroom was cold, but that didn't seem to matter a bit where a certain body part was concerned. It was a damned inconvenient time to have a hard on.

"He could have shot me," she said quietly. The trembling had stopped, but she didn't relinquish her hold on him. "He pointed the gun right at me. He held it against my neck. He could have shot any one of us."

"But he didn't. And you stayed calm. You were really brave, Cass."

"I was terrified. I just kept thinking that if I was quiet, no one would get hurt. And that I'd do whatever I could to make sure I didn't go with him."

"You did everything right."

"Then why am I so scared? If it's over and I'm fine, why doesn't it feel over?"

There was a plaintive note in her voice and he closed his eyes. "Because it's too new, and you're still processing it all. It takes time."

"I feel like such a wimp." She finally sat up a little. Not much; their bodies still touched in places and his arms were looped loosely around her. But she wasn't burrowed into the hollow of his neck any longer, with her breasts pressed against his chest.

"You're not a wimp." He leaned back and looked into her face. He could barely see her in the dark, but the numbers on the ancient clock radio gave enough light that he could make out her shadowy features and how her lower lip quivered just a little.

Damn, she knew how to make it difficult.

He lifted his hand and put it gently along the curve of her face, rubbing his thumb along the crest of her cheekbone. "You're not a wimp," he repeated, trying not to think about how soft her hair was against his knuckles. But she leaned into his touch and her eyelids fluttered closed. It was wrong that he wanted her so much. He tried to remember that she was here in an "official" capacity. It didn't seem to matter at all. Her eyes opened, her lips parted a little, and his gaze dropped to her mouth. "Cass," he murmured.

She didn't answer. She simply tilted her head the tiniest bit, drifting closer. An unmistakable invitation. Against his better judgment, he lowered his head and touched his lips to hers.

Sweet Jesus. Her lips were warm, soft, and tasted like sugared whiskey. She responded, molding her mouth to his, meeting his tongue tentatively, then with more confidence as she melted into him.

He hadn't thought he could get much harder. He'd been wrong.

"Mmm," she murmured against his mouth, destroying any rational thought he might have had of ending the kiss. He nibbled on her lower lip and she gasped, her body straining against his. The flannel was soft, just like the rest of her, and he moved his hand from her face and slid it down, down, to find the curve of her bottom. He lifted and shifted her body until she was straddling him, his feet on the floor and her ankles looped behind his back.

"Oh God," she moaned, and he moved his hips just a little. "Joe. Oh."

She tilted her head back and he tasted the soft skin of her neck. But that didn't last long as she leaned forward again, her hair falling over his shoulder as she kissed his jaw and licked along his earlobe. She smiled along his jawline and he was reminded of her saucy half-grin, the one she used when she was teasing. She'd been hiding her inner vixen behind a veneer of sweet politeness, hadn't she? Her tongue took another lick at his ear and he shivered with pleasure. It took a lot to surprise Joe, but she'd done it in about ten seconds flat.

He was going to explode if she wasn't careful. Her hands moved over the bare skin of his back. "You're so warm, Joe. So hard. Mmmm."

He scrambled to think of whether or not he had any condoms.

Her fingers moved to her pajama top and started undoing buttons. She was still wearing her bra underneath the top, and he reached behind her back and undid the clasp. She didn't even have the top off when he reached for her breast, fitting it into his palm. She made another small sound and pressed herself more firmly into his hand. God, she was going to be the death of him if she wasn't careful.

"Cass, we should stop. This... I shouldn't be doing this." He hated saying the words. They went completely against everything he was feeling right now.

"Not yet," she answered, urgency painting her words. "Touch me, Joe. I feel so alive when you touch me. I need to feel alive so badly."

He could do better than that. He tightened his arm around her hips, pulling her flush against his erection, then dipped his head and pulled her nipple into his mouth.

She cried out, the sound of it echoing through the cabin.

Things got even hotter, their movements fevered and frantic. He laved at her breasts with his tongue, loving the feel of her hard nipples nearly as much as he loved the way she ground her hips against him. But he wanted better access to her skin, wanted to taste more of her, so he flipped her onto her back on the bed and dropped onto his elbow beside her. She gave a little squeak at the abrupt motion, but then that hint of a smile curved her lips again as she reached down and touched him through his shorts.

"I want you," she said. "So bad I might die from it."

Holy hell. He struggled to think rationally. They barely knew each other; they were more acquaintances than good friends. He was in a position of authority. She was vulnerable. He couldn't sleep with her. *He couldn't.* And yet he could already feel what it would be like: hot, tight, perfect.

She didn't really want *him*, anyway. She wanted the outlet. She wanted to feel alive and vital. To counter the fear and helplessness she'd felt today. It was just part of her reaction, wasn't it? And one of them had to think with their brains.

Her hand stroked and his eyes damned near rolled back in his head.

He wouldn't make love to her. He wouldn't go that far. But he could give her what she really craved, and that was just as good. Well, almost as good. No sense lying to himself about that.

He fastened his mouth on her nipple again and her body jerked. Damn, she liked that, and he took his time driving her crazy with his tongue. But he found something she liked better. He slid his hand down inside her pajamas, inside the soft panties, and touched her. To his surprise, she parted her knees automatically, granting him full access—a surprising gift that made him regret having to do the right thing.

Joe paused to strip her bottoms off and then dropped them on the floor. Now she was completely naked on top of the blankets, and just the thin cotton of his underwear separated them. Her skin felt so good against his, and tasted even better. He kissed her again, long and slow and deep, while trailing his fingers over her breasts, her ribs, the soft skin of her stomach, her tender inner thighs.

She kissed him back, meeting him halfway, her hand trailing over his shoulder.

He slid his mouth away from hers, and instead left a wet trail of kisses down her neck, her collarbone, over her full breasts, her navel. All the while he teased her with his fingers until she reached down, grabbed his wrist, and thrust his fingers inside her.

This was what she wanted, then, and he was happy to accommodate. Keeping his gaze on her face, he used his hand to lift her to the breaking point. He could tell when she was getting close;

her hips met his thrusts with quick little jerks, and her head tossed on the pillow. He lowered his head and pulled one tight, pebbled nipple into his mouth and she came apart with strident moans as her legs clamped around his hand.

So much passion. And so much trust. He was awed and amazed and so turned on he reached down inside his shorts, his fingers damp, and finished the job in six firm pumps.

When he opened his eyes, she was watching him, her gaze dark and intense in the gray light. "You didn't want to..." She couldn't seem to finish the words, but he knew what she was thinking.

"Oh, I wanted to. But it would have been wrong, Cass. Shit, what we just did was so far out of professional bounds..."

"So what?"

He got off the bed, stripped off his underwear, and went to the dresser for a new pair. He slipped them on and then went back to the bed. It was cold now, and goose bumps erupted over his arms. He ignored them.

"The truth is, I would have felt like I was taking advantage of the situation." He rested his right hand on the mattress. "You had a nightmare. You had a traumatic day. There's feeling alive and then there's crossing a line."

She looked as if she were going to speak again, but he cut her off. "That doesn't mean I didn't want to. I did. So much it hurt."

He reached down and grabbed her top. "Here. You must be getting cold."

She sat up and he held the shirt for her while she put her arms in the sleeves. He swallowed thickly; when she opened her arms, her breasts were bare to his gaze and need stirred within him all over again. Damn, she was beautiful. All creamy skin, delicate pink tips, and full lips that looked puffy from the way she'd bitten down on them. As tenderly as he could, he buttoned the shirt to the second-last button, then handed her the bottoms and helped slide them over her slim hips. "There. All put back together."

"Thanks."

"Okay, then." He stood and paused, knowing he had to go back to the sofa, unsure of how to gracefully exit the situation. "Are you going to be okay now?"

She pulled the blankets close to her chest. "I don't know. Could... could you stay? Not for anything more like...Oh, shit. This is so awkward. I just..."

She looked away, but he knew that expression. It was uncertainty and fear. He'd seen it lots of times over the years. She didn't want to be alone. She'd had a gun pointed at her face today. Of course she was scared.

"It's okay," she said, her voice wobbling. "I know I'm safe now. Go back to sleep. I'm sorry I woke you."

He sat back on the edge of the bed. "Wrong or right, I'm not sorry," he said. "Not sorry at all. If you want me to stay, I'll stay. If it'll make you feel safer."

She nodded quickly, a few brief bobs of her head but he could see the relief as she relaxed her shoulders.

He shifted and lifted the covers, then slipped beneath the blankets. It was warm inside, thanks to her body heat, and she scooted over a bit so there was room for him.

"Damn. Hang on." He crawled out of bed again and went to the living room to retrieve his pillow. When he came back, she was fully over on one side of the bed, and she'd turned back the covers for him to get in.

"You're sure this isn't too awkward, Joe? I mean...oh, I don't know what I mean."

He smiled at her uncertainty. "It's been a day of odd circumstances. If you'd told me this morning that we'd be sharing a bed together tonight, I would have called you a liar. But I want you to feel safe. And we both need some sleep. It's okay, really."

"Thanks."

No thanks required. It wasn't exactly a hardship, curling up next to a warm, beautiful woman. Then again, it wasn't exactly an easy thing to do, either. Especially now. Even though they hadn't made love, the scent of sex lingered in the air. He knew how she felt, how she tasted. They'd blown way past platonic and plunged deep into intimate territory.

Joe put down the pillow and got under the covers again, rolling to his side to face her. "You're safe, Cassidy. I promise."

"I know that, in my head. I think you're right. The dream was just me still processing what happened. It's the most afraid I've ever been, you know?"

He did know. The first time he'd faced an armed man, he'd frozen for a moment. It was hard to face mortality straight-on. Her words gave him comfort, too, in an odd way. If that was as afraid as she'd ever been, then maybe her married life hadn't been as bad as he'd imagined.

"Come here," he murmured, and scooted closer. He reached around and pulled her next to his body, spoon-fashion, so that her head rested on his lower shoulder and her feet tangled with his. Her bottom lightly touched his hips; he'd have to be careful there. Even the slightest touch could bring his arousal back to life.

"You're so warm."

"You are too."

She reached behind for his hand, then drew it over her hips so that his palm rested on the soft flatness of her belly. "You have big hands."

He smiled in the darkness. "You know what they say about big hands."

"Big gloves," she replied, and he felt her smile.

He closed his eyes and let out a breath.

"I feel safe with you, Joe."

Me too, he almost said, but that was a ridiculous thought. Why would he need someone to make him feel safe? He thought back to that day at her apartment, when he'd dealt with Darren and his ugly, angry face. Cassidy had tried to look more angry than afraid, but he'd been able to tell. She'd been intimidated and unsure. That she was even considering dating again was a leap of faith.

And her first foray into dating had turned into a disaster. Well, at least as far as the dating site was concerned. In other ways...

He was going to ask her about the online dating thing when he noticed her breathing had deepened. "Cass?" he whispered, but she didn't move. She'd fallen asleep, curled up in his arms, warm and trusting.

Sleep took a long time for Joe, though. He held still, afraid to move and wake her. Her hair held the faint scent of her shampoo—something light and floral. His hands already itched to touch her again. Maybe they hadn't known each other well before tonight, but unique circumstances had unexpected effects. Things had changed. She'd opened up to him, and he'd let her in, too. More than she realized.

He wanted nothing more than to touch her again, to slip inside her, feel her tighten around him. But until this Chad guy was in custody, he wouldn't. He'd already breached any sort of professionalism he possessed; this was the one line he wouldn't cross.

But then, once this was over...all bets were off.

Chapter Six

C assidy squinted against the shaft of sunlight beaming through the bedroom window.

She was in Joe's cabin. In the woods. In his bed. And... Memory came flooding back and her face flamed. He'd been in his bed, too. With her. And they'd...

Well, they hadn't. She shifted her head on the pillow, thankful she was alone under the covers right now. She hadn't heard him get up, but as she woke fully, she was aware of sounds coming from the kitchen.

Thank God she had her pajamas on.

There was a small clanging sound, and the hiss of a kettle heating. Cassidy remained motionless, trying to process everything she remembered from the night. There'd been the terror of the dream, where she'd stared at the man she now knew was named Chad, and he'd smiled before pulling the trigger pointed at her head. She'd awakened screaming, only to find Joe at her side, dressed in nothing but some cotton shorts.

He'd been so warm. So alive and solid and reassuring. So strong and sexy and she'd clung to him, needing to feel that contact when inside she'd turned to ice.

But nothing had prepared her for the heat of his kisses, the touch of his rough fingers on her skin, his mouth on her body.

Abandon. She'd let herself go without a second thought, something so uncharacteristic it was shocking. Or might have been if the memory of it wasn't so sweet. He'd been turned on, too. She felt an ache between her legs as she thought of how he'd reached inside his briefs...she wished now they'd made love.

One-nighters were not her style. But sometimes an opportunity was too good to miss.

"You're awake."

Her gaze snapped to the doorway, where he stood with a mug in his hand. Was she still blushing? God, she hoped not. Her whole body felt flushed and she tried to smile as naturally as possible.

"What time is it?"

He looked at his watch. "Oh, around nine-thirty. Are you hungry? What do you take in your coffee?"

She pushed herself up to a sitting position, leaving the blankets covering her to her hips. "Nine-thirty? I never sleep this late."

"It was a...um...a weird night. No more nightmares?"

Hah. She'd slept like a baby after their roll in the sheets. "None," she said quietly. "And yeah, I could eat." She smiled again. "I like milk, no sugar."

He came inside the bedroom and held out the cup. "I guessed."

When she took the mug from his hand, their fingers brushed and the contact sent little darts of awareness through her. "Thanks," she murmured, wondering how on earth this was going to stop being awkward. She hid her face by taking a sip. She wasn't sure if Joe could really cook, but she was reminded of her aversion to instant coffee. It was hot and strong, at least.

"I've got stuff ready for omelets if you're up to it. There's time for a quick shower if you like, too. Or you can wait until after breakfast."

She'd feel better if she faced him across the breakfast table wearing regular clothes. "I wouldn't mind a quick shower."

"I put out a towel for you already. Breakfast in fifteen?"

Her stomach growled in response and she laughed a little, pressing a hand to her belly. "I think that sounds perfect."

He disappeared out the door again and she flipped back the covers and stepped out onto the wood floor.

As she dug around in her overnight bag, she heard Joe in the kitchen, humming something as he cooked. It had been a long time since she'd heard morning sounds like this; she'd been living alone for nearly a year now. Sometimes the solitude was great, but sometimes it was nice to think of someone being there. Just there, cooking breakfast or watching the TV or...hell. She might as well face it. She was pretty lonely. The fact that she'd signed up for an online dating service was proof enough of that.

The water was hot with lots of pressure, and she closed her eyes and tilted her head back, letting it cascade through her hair and down her back. She soaped her arms and ran the suds over her breasts, unable to stop thinking about Joe touching them last night. He'd known how to do everything just right.

Her hand drifted lower, rinsing away the slippery soap. Would she go home today? Had they caught the guy? What would happen if she had to stay another night?

She turned off the shower and got out, toweled off quickly, wrapped the towel around her hair, and got dressed. Jeans, a narrow T-shirt, and then a looser fleece hoodie over top—certainly nothing sexy or seductive about it. She squeezed extra moisture out of her hair and hung up the towel, then brushed out the mass and ran her fingers through it, shaking it out. She'd forgotten a hair dryer and Joe wasn't likely to have one. Oh well. If he kept the fire stoked, it shouldn't take long to dry.

Joe was sliding a semi-circle of omelet onto a plate just as she walked into the kitchen.

"You didn't have to do this, you know." She smiled at him, determined to put things on an even footing this morning. There was no denying that yesterday had been an extraordinary circumstance. "Though I appreciate it. It smells amazing." It was a treat to have a man cook for her, too. She owned a restaurant and usually ended up doing a lot of the cooking no matter what the situation. She liked that he was wasn't intimidated by that.

"I like to cook. Good thing, too, because otherwise I'd go pretty hungry up here." He handed her the plate. "Not like I can stop at the corner fast food place and grab a burger, you know?"

She went to the table as he put food for himself on another plate. It wasn't just the fluffy omelet, but there was also a heap of pan fries, crispy on the outside, punctuated with fried onions. Her mouth watered and she picked up her fork. At the first bite she closed her eyes. Ham, peppers, and mushrooms, if her guess was correct. And not regular cheese, either. It had a kick to it—Pepper Jack, maybe? The eggs were fluffy and perfectly done.

"Oh, my sweet Lord," she said, stabbing a piece of potato. "You weren't kidding. This is delicious."

"I thought you could use a good breakfast. Dinner last night was hit and miss, I gather. And you're going to want a full stomach this morning."

She frowned, hesitated with her fork in mid-air. "I am?"

He nodded and grinned. "I'm going to take you on a hike."

A hike. She sat back in her chair. It would definitely give them something to do today other than sitting in the cabin, staring at each other. "I take it I can't go home, then?"

Joe frowned and shook his head. "No, they still haven't caught him. I checked in with Sam and Tim first thing this morning. But we know a lot more. He's divorced, in a fair bit of debt, and overdue on his child support payments. He's got a previous arrest for assault, though the charges were dropped. It sounds like it was just a bar fight when he was younger."

Cassidy wasn't sure she was still hungry.

"It's good, though. It sounds like he's more of a guy who's at the end of his rope, you know? It's just a matter of if he recognized you, or if he realized that you recognized him. That's why I suggested to NMFR that they disable your profile last night. I didn't want him to come across your picture and put it all together. We'll keep looking, but if he thinks it's safe, he'll come home. Probably catch up on his child support to avoid getting in trouble."

"If he's not dangerous, then I could go home."

"Except we don't know for sure that he didn't recognize you." Joe frowned. "If you really want to go home, I'll take you tomorrow. Monday I can put a regular staffer on you. And, uh, I promise that nothing like last night will happen again."

Well damn. That was disappointing. Probably smart, but a letdown just the same. "That wasn't your fault, Joe." She stared at her plate.

"It certainly wasn't yours. I took advantage."

She looked up, startled. "What? No. If anyone took advantage, it was me."

"Nice try." He smiled a little and picked up his coffee. "I'm supposed to be the one looking after you."

"And you did," she replied, butterflies of anticipation fluttering around in her stomach. "Better than any calming tea or whiskey or sleeping pill."

His gaze clung to hers. "This is the damnedest thing."

"Isn't it?" She smiled back, and then attempted to resume eating, though she wasn't really tasting the food. She was too attuned to Joe, sitting there in his jeans and soft cotton shirt, looking ruggedly delicious. "Hey, at least I can promise that I won't run out part way through the meal and stiff you with the bill. That puts me head and shoulders above your last date."

"I'm never going to live that down, am I?" "I wouldn't tease you about it if I thought it would really upset you. It doesn't, does it?"

He shook his head. "Nope. But I've told my sister that she is not allowed to set me up on a date ever again. I can find my own dates."

"Indeed." She sent him a teasing look, then focused on her plate. He was quiet so long that she looked over again. "What is it?"

"Nothing." He shook himself out of whatever he was thinking and shoved a huge forkful of potatoes into his mouth. He stood and gathered his plate, then went to the sink to scrape the remnants into the garbage before stacking the dishes. "Do you think you could be ready in ten minutes or so? The morning's warming up, and we can be there during the nicest part of the day."

She scrambled to eat what was on her plate; it was too good to waste and she really was hungry. "Be where?" she asked between bites.

"It's a surprise. But you'll like it. And it'll take your mind off the other stuff. Trust me. I go there a lot when I want to clear my head."

They'd set out on foot a good half hour earlier, following the dirt road for a few hundred yards and then veering off to the left, going single file down a rough trail that led to a gully. The leaves were changing now, morphing from green to gold and rust, and the sun shining through the branches seemed to gild everything with a hazy glow. Cassidy was content to let Joe lead the way; his reassuring footsteps and imposing figure were steady and sure, and now and again he looked back to make sure she was following close behind. Like he did now, flashing her a quick grin.

"Doing okay?"

"Of course." She'd thrown a windbreaker over her hoodie, just in case the mountain air cooled, and she was glad she'd brought running shoes with her. Boots would have been better, but the path, though narrow, wasn't overly rocky or uneven.

"It widens out soon. ATVs have a trail through here. Then it won't be so rough."

"I like it. I haven't been out like this for a long time."

She hadn't. She'd been in town, or at work, and she hadn't made time to get out into nature much.

"I keep saying I'm going to get a dog," Joe confessed. "But with my hours…I don't want to leave him or her alone all day. Sometimes, in bad weather, I crash at the station rather than try to come up the mountain. It wouldn't be fair."

"I know what you mean. We had a dog, you know." Just saying it made her unbearably sad. She missed Pete. But it would have been difficult to keep him with her hours, and besides, her landlord didn't allow pets. Pete got to stay with Darren and the bimbo.

"Had?" Joe's gaze met hers. "Was custody a part of the divorce?"

He said it seriously; there was no sarcasm in his tone whatsoever. She nodded. "Yeah. The house was all set up for him anyway, with a dog run in the back, and no pets are allowed at the apartment."

"Do you miss him?"

Her throat clogged a bit. After all this time, it was the dog that made her emotional. Go figure. "I do. I miss having him there when I come home. Or sleeping at the foot of the bed."

She wanted to change the subject, so she took a deep breath and moved on. "So, do you think you'll always live up here?"

The path widened into the ATV trail he'd mentioned. She took a few jogging steps and moved up beside him, and their pace slowed a bit.

He looked over at her and gave a little shrug. "I don't know. I love it, but sometimes it'd be more convenient to be closer to town."

"Oh, I don't think you should give it up," she replied, taking a deep breath of crisp autumn air. "It's too nice. Maybe you'll figure something out."

"Maybe."

Their footsteps made crunchy noises on the trail, and birds peeped and sang from the trees. Occasionally a puff of wind came along and rattled the leaves, a sound that seemed particular to fall, as if the foliage was paper-thin and vulnerable.

"So where are we going?"

He looked over and grinned again. "Can't you just enjoy the journey?"

"Well, I am." She smiled back. "But I'm wondering how far it is and if I'm going to be sore tomorrow because you brought a pack. And are we going to meet any bears out here or anything?"

"You never know. If something happens, though, I don't have to outrun the bear."

"You don't?" Her eyes widened. Had he brought his gun with him? Bear spray?

He chuckled. "Nope. I just have to outrun you."

Her mouth fell open and she gave his arm a shove. "Jerk."

His laugh echoed through the trees. "Haven't you heard that one before?"

"What can I say? I've lived a sheltered life."

His laughter died away. "Have you really, Cass? Was Darren always...did he hurt you?"

She hesitated, the lightness of the mood gone. Regret settled like a rock in the pit of her stomach. "Not in any way that you could see," she replied quietly. She kept walking, determined to keep her tone conversational rather than stop and make a whole big deal out of it.

"He just...wore me down, I guess. Made me feel like things were always my fault. Like I wasn't good enough. I believed him for a while." She laughed, but it was a humorless sound. "Until I caught him cheating. And I was smart enough to figure out that if he could lie about *that*, he was probably lying about everything else. And I kicked his sorry ass out."

"Except..."

"Except he's still really angry. He still thinks he should have a say in my life. Maybe he thinks he can intimidate me."

"And can he? Are you scared?"

She stopped, and her chest cramped a little. "Sometimes. But I get through it. I can't let him bully me." Her breath shook as she inhaled. "As much as I wanted a family, I'm glad there aren't any kids in the middle and that I don't need to go to him for financial support. The restaurant's doing well, and I'm self-sufficient. It'll never make me rich, but I don't care."

"Was it a big deal to leave the restaurant behind for the weekend? I never thought..."

She shook her head. "I called my manager before we left the station last night. She's going to keep everything going while I'm away. I hired good people and I trust them."

Joe reached over and took her hand and she finally looked up at him. His eyes were so honest, so caring. He made her feel safe just by holding her hand. And it wasn't only his size, or the reassuring sight of him in his rugged boots and plaid fleece. Though that didn't hurt —it was just as sexy as his uniform.

"I'm sorry you've had to deal with so much. If you ever need back up, I want you to call me. I'll help. I promise."

That made her go all warm inside. "That's sweet, Joe. But after this weekend, I'll be back at my place and you'll be back at work. I'm fine, really."

He squeezed her fingers. "The offer still stands. For as long as you need it."

She knew he meant it. And it meant more—not less—knowing he was the kind of man who would offer that same assistance to anyone who needed it. "Thanks."

He pulled on her hand, and they started walking again. "We're almost there," he said, picking up the pace. "Can you hear it?"

She didn't know what she was supposed to be hearing, and the sound of their feet on the dirt didn't help, but it didn't take long before she made out a rushing sound, like wind, only it was steady and constant. "Water? Is there a creek here or something?"

"Better." He grinned. "Come on."

They left the main trail and started down a narrower path. They only went about fifty feet when the forest opened up and the creek that had flowed perpendicular to the trail made close to a ninety-degree turn and tumbled over an outcropping of granite. They were situated just off the bank, about half-way down, so they could see the water cascade from above, and the calmer pool at the bottom as it meandered again down the side of the mountain.

"Wow," she breathed, putting her hands on her hips. "This is seriously pretty."

"I know. It's bigger in the spring, during the melt." He led her over to a couple of large rocks, resting in what might have been a root system from a tree years earlier. "Have a seat. Close your eyes and just listen."

She perched on the rock and obediently closed her eyes. The sound of the water filled her ears, the rush of it constant and soothing. As her attention deepened, she made out the slightly different sound of the wind in the leaves and the distinctive calls of birds. She wished the rock were big enough for her to lie on her back and stare up at the sky. She made do with tilting her head back and she opened her eyes. The birches and pines made a canopy above her head, all green and gold against the pale blue of the sky.

The best part was that Joe didn't say a thing. She looked over and he simply sat, his elbows on his knees, and watched the water. He was perfectly content.

And she was here with him, because he'd brought her.

Yesterday they'd been acquaintances. Today they were so much more. It had little to do with what had happened in his bedroom last night. It was deeper. Like they were the same sort of person, deep down where it mattered.

It was that knowledge that had her leaning forward and shifting off her rock. She ignored the cool, damp earth beside his perch; she knelt on the spongy forest floor and looked up at him.

"Cassidy?"

She didn't say anything. She just pulled herself up a little taller and leaned in to kiss him.

His lips were cold, but not for long. The inside of his mouth was warm, and they kissed long and deep, taking their time. She didn't want to rush. She wanted to savor every single moment they were together. Joe had put his hands into his pockets...to keep from reaching for her, perhaps? She smiled a little and put her hand on his thigh for balance. And the kiss went on, and on, and on...

When every nerve ending in her body was begging for more, she backed away. Joe's eyes were dazed and she loved that she was the cause of it. "What's in the bag?" she asked softly, and nearly laughed when he finally blinked and came to his senses.

"Shit." He shook his head. "You do that to a man and then ask him what's in his backpack?"

"I wanted to kiss you, that's all."

"You sure did a good job."

Joe was very good at giving her back some of her lost confidence. "Thanks."

"I'm still supposed to be doing a job, you know."

"We're on a hike, Joe." She smiled and reached around him for the bag.

"That was so you wouldn't be bored."

She laughed and searched for the zipper. "I could say the same."

"Give me that. You're becoming a pain in my ass, Cassidy Strong."

She lifted her chin and met his gaze. "I didn't hear you complaining." Damned if he didn't blush a little, and she grinned. "Besides, who's going to know? I'm not going to tell."

Their gazes held. There was something about what she'd just said that resonated between them. Yes, she might be disillusioned when it came to relationships, but she was still smart enough to know that sometimes the forbidden was pretty exciting. Today her need wasn't reactive. It wasn't because of a bad dream or wanting to feel alive, though she did want that, and there was no question that Joe made her feel that way. But today was lighter. More fun. After today she might not get another chance to see where this could lead.

They munched on trail mix bars and water and the sky began to cloud over as afternoon settled in. With the cloud came lower temperatures, and they finally left the waterfall behind and started back to the trail and the cabin. They didn't talk much, but they didn't need to fill the silence with chatter; it was comfortable and easy. As they neared the clearing, Cassidy hung back and watched Joe walk ahead. He was right. He should have a dog. She could just imagine him with a hound or a black lab or something, trotting at his heels.

Once they were back inside, Joe stirred the embers in the stove and added wood to get it going again. Cassidy took off her sneakers—slightly muddy now—and left them at the door. She looked down at her jeans. There were two round, damp spots where she'd knelt on the ground. She'd have to put on something else.

"I'm going to go change," she announced. Once in his room, she rummaged through her bag for a pair of yoga pants. "Any word from the station?"

"None yet," he called back, and she heard him shut the door on the stove. She shivered as she pulled on the pants. Her shirt was long-sleeved, but the fresh air and the cool cabin made her feel like she'd never warm up.

"Hey Joe, do you have an old hoodie or something I can put on over top of my shirt?"He came to the door. "In the closet, on the shelf. Take your pick."

She chose an oversized one in light gray. It was baggy and soft and smelled like him and she cuddled inside it for a moment before going back out into the living room. Joe was in the kitchen and she heard the breathy sound of a kettle being heated.

"I thought you might like something hot to drink," he suggested.

"That sounds awesome." She smiled at him, suddenly aware that they were alone again, with no one to interrupt them. It was like they were the only two people in the world. The possibilities were endless. Perhaps the magnitude of that thought was what held her back for the moment. Endless possibility could be a bit scary in reality.

"I got a text from Sam. Our guy deposited the money in a bank in Silverton last night. Then he logged onto his banking site at a Wi-Fi hot spot and transferred his child support. It looks like he's heading back toward Greeley. Sam's pretty sure they'll pick him up soon. You won't have anything to worry about."

"That's good news. Why on earth would he use a bank, though?" She frowned, and reached into the cupboard for two mugs. "Wouldn't he want to keep the money hidden?"

Joe shrugged and grabbed a can of hot chocolate. "He paid his child support through a transfer. That's probably for an official trail of the payment. He deposited just over two grand. The bank said he got less than five, so there's still some money unaccounted for."

She looked up at Joe and shook her head. "He risked a lot for a little bit of money. The penalty for armed robbery has got to be way more than defaulting on support."

"Maybe he thought he'd get more." He got a spoon out of the drawer.

"Maybe he was just desperate." She shuddered, thinking of his harsh voice and the way he'd waved the gun around. "Desperation makes people do weird things." She should know. Darren had gone crazy when she'd first told him she'd seen a divorce lawyer. She still had the threatening e-mails and texts.

She scooped powder into the mugs and once the kettle clicked off, she poured the water. Joe stirred. "Sorry. No marshmallows."

She grinned. "The fact that you even have hot chocolate says something."

"Wait. I have an idea." He went to a cupboard and took down a small bottle. "Irish cream. It's great in hot chocolate."

He added a dollop to each cup and Cassidy took a sip. "Mmm. Delicious."

"So." They took their cups to the living room. Joe sat in the chair, leaving the sofa for Cassidy. It looked like today he was going to keep his professional distance. Sure, he'd kissed her back at the waterfall, but she'd been the one to initiate it.

"So," she answered, smiling over the rim of her cup.

"What would you like to do tonight? We could watch a movie. And I do get a couple of basic channels. There's probably a hockey game on."

What would she like to do? She looked over at Joe and dared herself not to think about last night in his bed. Of course, she'd never been good at dares. And the shot of liquor warmed its way through her stomach and made her relax.

What I'd really like to do, Joe, is start with kissing you, then taking off your clothes. Then taking off my clothes and the two of us soaking in a hot bubble bath, our limbs slippery and soft. Then I'd take you to the bed and make sweet love to you all night long. Screw the movie.

As if she'd ever actually say that.

But…

He wasn't going to make the first move. But why not make the most of the forced isolation? He could have put her up in a motel. Assigned another officer to her and worked the overtime. Why hadn't he?

"A movie sounds good. And dinner. Maybe I can cook for you tonight."

"You're welcome to raid the pantry, such as it is."

"Deal."

They sipped in silence for a bit, and then curiosity got the better of her. "Why don't you have a girlfriend, Joe? Because trust me, you're way too eligible to be spending your weekends alone up here with just the trees and bears for company. And I'm not talking about the failed blind date. I mean…if you wanted, you could snag a woman like that." She snapped her fingers for emphasis.

He chuckled, down low. "I had one, once. I had a wife, actually. Got married right after school. It didn't work out."

Holy shit. Joe was divorced?

"What happened?"

He shrugged. "Aw, hell. We were just too young. Thought we knew what we wanted. It turned out she didn't want to be married to a cop. Too much worry. Weird hours. She wasn't…well, she wasn't the center of attention all the time." He sighed. "That makes her sound like she was selfish, and she wasn't, not really. She just...well, I don't think she was independent enough to handle it, and I didn't want to change. I love what I do." He sighed. "I didn't put her first."

Heavy. And not as easy a decision as, say, someone cheating with a younger, cheaper piece on the side.

"I'm sorry."

"Eh. It's water under the bridge now." He took another drink of chocolate. "I think I realized that if I ever get married again, it would have to be to someone who isn't afraid to have their own life."

She smiled softly. "Okay, so I'm going to confess something here and you're not allowed to laugh. I've actually watched *The Princess Diaries*." At his confused expression, she elaborated. "It's a book that was made into a movie. Well, two movies. Anyway, in the second movie, Amelia's mother tells Amelia that being married is about being herself, but with someone else. It's meant to be confusing and quirky, but I've always thought it was really insightful. To me, marriage is about two complete individuals choosing to share their lives with each other. They're the same people, but they're with someone else, and that bond makes them more. Does that make sense?"

"It does. I think. Like you shouldn't have to change who you are in order to be with someone. You shouldn't lose your own identity."

"Yeah, well, it's great in theory. I'm not sure I really buy into it." She was just thinking about dating again. Marriage wasn't even close to being on her radar.

He smiled at her. "Hell, what a heavy conversation. This is what happens when you don't have cable."

"Or internet."

He laughed. "Or that."

Her limbs were deliciously relaxed, but she didn't want to fall asleep. "So, about this dinner...anything you have in mind?"

His gaze caught hers. "Surprise me."

And just like that, the air hummed between them.

She might. She just might.

Chapter Seven

Joe listened to the sounds in the kitchen and tried to stop thinking about how Cassidy tasted. He distracted himself by remembering the sound of her voice, but then he recalled her soft, sexy laugh and realized how flawed his strategy was. Maybe he should just think about how she looked in the plain yoga pants and hoodie. But when she'd gotten up from the sofa to go to the kitchen, he'd got a good look at her perky ass. And the hoodie was his. It probably smelled like her now, all soft and flowery and feminine.

Damn, he was weak.

"Joe? You got garlic?"

He shook his head. "In a jar in the fridge. The minced kind."

"Thanks."

She was just making dinner.

But earlier this afternoon she'd been on her knees in front of him, teasing him with her soft, full lips and it had taken all his willpower to not tip her over onto the bed of golden leaves. He was doing a job, dammit. But last night had made a joke out of that idea. He'd slept beside her. She'd fallen asleep and he could have got up and gone back to the couch, but he hadn't. He'd curled his body around her and slept like a baby. Like she belonged there.

He was rapidly losing his self-respect.

His phone buzzed, and he looked at the display. It was Sam again. But it was a call, not a text, and he hit the answer button and got up, heading for the bedroom and some privacy.

Five minutes later he sat on the bed, holding the phone in his hands, wondering what to do.

The guy was in custody. There was no longer any reason to keep Cassidy here, under his protection. As a lawman, he should tell her, drive her back into town, and deliver her to her apartment, with assurances that she'd be contacted by victim services and to expect to be subpoenaed to testify.

As a man, he didn't want her to leave. He wanted...

He wanted her.

"Joe? Where'd you go? Dinner's almost ready." Her voice called from the kitchen, shaking him out of his thoughts.

What the hell was he going to do? The right thing? Or what felt right? And why did the two options have to be so at odds with each other?

Cassidy stepped back and took a deep inhale, suddenly nervous.

The small drop-leaf table was set for two, with plates, wine glasses, and, for lack of a better alternative, paper towels folded as napkins. She'd found a couple of thick candles in a drawer and she'd put them in the middle of the table, their soft glow flickering through the small space. Joe didn't have a huge stock of groceries, but she'd managed to find a few chicken breasts, a box of spaghetti noodles, and a can of diced tomatoes. He did keep fresh vegetables, so she'd put together a basic marinara to go with the pasta, cooked the chicken in olive oil, garlic, and basil, and sliced some crusty bread from a French loaf she'd found in the freezer and had put in the ancient toaster oven. She'd brushed each slice with olive oil and broiled it until it was golden. All in all, it wasn't bad for a thrown-together meal.

And there was wine. She'd found a single bottle of Chianti in the pantry. There was a tag on it—from last Christmas.

She wanted him to like it; for supper to be the first step to the rest of the evening. An evening that she hoped ended with Joe *not* sleeping on the sofa. Her life had kind of sucked for the last several months. There wasn't any reason why she shouldn't take advantage of a good opportunity. If...

If he wanted to. It was up to Joe, in the end. She knew what she wanted. Maybe she'd even suspected when she'd given him that cheesecake after his failed date. Maybe it had just taken this...forced proximity for her to realize it.

His footsteps sounded on the floor and she caught her breath, pressed her hands to her cheeks. *Get your shit together, girl,* she cautioned herself. *You're not sixteen anymore.*

"Wow."

Joe stopped in the doorway to the kitchen, surprise blanking his face for a moment. He looked up at her, his grayish-green eyes wide with wonder. "You found all this in my cupboards?"She grinned. "I'm very resourceful."

"Clearly."

She held up the bottle of wine. "Do you want a glass?"

His face shadowed as she asked, and she put down the bottle. "Sorry. You don't like it? It's been in there for a long time, right? I should have known."

"It's not that."

"What's wrong?" He looked so serious that she was sure it was something bad, and her stomach did a slow twist.

"Sam called back. They've made the arrest."

Relief flooded her body and she smiled. "That's great!"He smiled back, his shoulders relaxing. "Yes, it is. He didn't put up any resistance, either. The rest of the money, the gun...it was all in his car."

"He didn't think he'd get caught?"

"They're interrogating him now. But it doesn't look as if he recognized you from the site. I think he thought he'd got away with it."

"That's very good news." So why was he looking so pensive?

"It means...you don't need my protection anymore."

She looked at the wine bottle, uncorked and not poured. She'd made dinner. There was a movie. Only...

"We shouldn't let the food go to waste," she said, the words sounding thin to her ears. "I can re-cork the wine, I guess."

"Dinner looks wonderful. I just...I mean, I brought you here to make sure you were safe. We didn't really know who we were dealing with at first, you know? But now..."

"Now duty tells you that you need to take me home. If I stay longer, it's not just business anymore. I get it, Joe." Her voice sounded flat.

So much for seduction.

"Cass..."

There was a note of longing in his voice that gave her the smallest bit of hope.

"Yes?"

His gaze touched hers again. "I'm trying to do what's right here."

"I can see that. So let's just sit, and eat, okay?"

He came over to her then. "Cass."

"What do you want me to say, Joe?" She lifted her head and met his gaze.

"I don't know. The truth."

She thought about that for a minute. Was either of them ready for the truth? She bit down on her lip as she considered, then lifted her chin and met his gaze evenly. "The truth is, that if you had a glass or two of wine, you wouldn't be able to drive, and I'd have to stay here until morning."

"Is that what *you* want?"

He was putting it all on her. All the responsibility, but also the choice. The fact that he hadn't immediately told her to pack her things and get ready to go spoke volumes. He wasn't saying no. He was leaving it up to her. When was the last time anyone considered her feelings, her wants, in this way?

When was the last time she'd really felt in charge...at least in her personal life?

In response, she picked up the wine bottle and filled each glass.

"Cass," he murmured.

"I don't want to go home tonight, Joe. I want to stay here. With you. Maybe it'll be watching a movie under a blanket on the sofa. Maybe it'll be something else. But this is where I want to be. Just for a few more hours. Daylight will be here soon enough, and reality with it. Let me escape for just a little longer."

Escape. She hadn't even known she'd been looking to get away. But wasn't she? Wasn't that what putting her profile on the dating site had been about? Experiencing something new and exciting...with a man who exhibited all the qualities she'd recently discovered in Joe Lawson?

Both times they'd kissed, she'd initiated the contact. But now Joe took the wine bottle from her hand and placed it on the table. His palm settled on her hip, and her breath caught as their bodies brushed. His gaze held hers for a long moment, but then dropped to her mouth.

It was like someone lit a match inside her. Her lips parted automatically, and Joe leaned in, kissing her softly, thoroughly, in the middle of the kitchen. It was the first kiss without the specter of the robbery suspect between them, and it felt different. More permissible. More...everything.

If he kept doing that, dinner was going to be a non-event.

As if he'd heard her thought, he backed off, making a little *mmm* sound against her lips as he finished the kiss. "Let's eat," he suggested.

Cassidy finished up the dishes as Joe brought in more wood for the stove. It had seemed like once they'd made the decision for her to stay, there was no rush for anything. They'd eaten, chatted, looked at each other over the soft candlelight, flirted.

Now, though, darkness had fallen outside, the meal was over, the kitchen tidied, and the evening stretched before them. She had her DVDs that she'd brought, but the thought of sitting on the sofa watching a chick flick wasn't exactly how she wanted to spend the night. She didn't want to watch the story unfold; she wanted to experience it for herself.

She hung the dishtowel on a hook and brushed her hands down her pants. The fear of yesterday was over. If anything, the news of the arrest brought relief and a strange energy to her body. Freedom, perhaps. And the notion that she was hidden away in a cabin with a very sexy lawman who seemed equally interested in her—and not just professionally.

The living room was quiet. She found Joe sitting on the sofa, his head against the back, his eyes closed and relaxed.

Cassidy finally admitted that she was rather partial to denim and flannel. Not that his uniform wasn't a turn-on, because it was, all starched and pressed and official-looking. But this...this was approachable and soft and hit all the right buttons.

She walked softly across the room, put one knee on the sofa cushion beside him, and lifted her other leg so that she straddled his lap.

"Well, hello," he said, his voice deep and lazy. He kept his eyes closed and she wanted to kiss his eyelashes, they were so pretty.

"Hello yourself," she replied. She shifted on his lap, and he chuckled.

"Cass, what are you doing?"

It was now or never. They'd made the choice. She'd had a little liquid courage with dinner. "Seducing you."

His lids lifted and his dazed eyes met hers. "Honey, you picked an easy target."

"Really?" *Damn.* She'd told herself she wasn't going to be insecure. And here she was, already asking for reassurance.

"Was there ever any doubt?" He ran his tongue over his bottom lip. "It's been torture all day. Why else did you think I took you out in the woods?"

"To show me the falls?" She shifted again, and felt him rise to meet her.

"To keep busy. To keep myself from doing what I really wanted."

She lifted her hand and ran her fingernail over his lip, down the slight cleft in his chin. "And what's that?"

His fingers captured hers. "Spending the day in bed with you. Very unprofessional, you see. The kind of thing that could get me in a lot of trouble."

"Oh, very unprofessional. With me being under your protection and all." She reached out and began sliding the buttons of his shirt out through the buttonholes. "But guess what?"

"What?" His hand settled on the curve of her hip, warm and wide, and stroked lightly. Even through her yoga pants, it felt heavenly.

"Since the arrest this afternoon, I'm not under your protection. I'm free as a bird. You could ravage me all night long and there wouldn't be a thing inappropriate about it." She let her fingers touch skin as she moved to the next button.

"Jesus, Cass. That's an idea to put in a man's head." The fingers on her hip tightened.

She stopped, looked him full in the face. "Sweetheart, that idea was already there, and you know it."

Now that was the confidence she'd hoped for. She smiled, then reached for the hem of the hoodie and pulled it over her head.

She was still wearing a T-shirt, but she caught Joe's gaze dropping to her chest. "I'm glad you stoked the fire," she purred, and pulled her shirt off, too. In for a penny...

Her skin erupted into goose bumps, first from the cold, and then from the feel of Joe's palm cupping her breast. Her hardened nipple pressed into his hand as she leaned forward to kiss him. This time there was little gentleness about it; the kiss was fuelled by need and desire and urgency. Tongues first, then teeth as Joe nibbled on her bottom lip before sliding to the curve of her neck. The wet touch was so delicious she gasped and moaned simultaneously. There was a slight popping feeling and then her bra gaped.

"One hand," she murmured, lost in sensation. "Talented."

"I have a few skills," he replied, his mouth hot against her shoulder. "Sit up for me, Cass."

She lifted a little and it put her breasts nearly level with his mouth. "Mmm," he murmured, and she watched, fascinated and utterly turned on as he circled a nipple with his tongue.

"More," she gasped, torn between pushing herself against him and pulling away. "Joe, stop. I want...I need..."

"What do you need?" he asked, pausing his motions briefly. But as soon as he asked, he went back to teasing and sucking and she cried out.

"I need to see you. To touch you. I need...I need everything."

She pushed away, the cool air hitting her damp breasts. She grabbed the throw from the chair and spread it haphazardly on the rug in front of the wood stove. Then she shimmied out of her yoga pants and panties so that she was standing buck naked in his living room. She marveled at how she didn't feel the least bit self-conscious. No, she was far too hot and needy to worry about that.

Joe cursed. Softly, succinctly, and she smiled. "Oh, I hope so," she replied, and her heart pounded painfully as he got up from the sofa and came toward her.

She pulled the tails of his shirt out of his jeans and then pushed the soft fabric off his shoulders. Damn, but he was fine. All broad shoulders and lean hips, just the way she liked. Next she undid the button on his jeans, and pushed them down over his hips along with his shorts—a task made slightly more difficult as they snagged on the way down.

And then they were both naked, and there was a moment in which the enormity of what was happening swept in and threatened to overwhelm her. Until he reached for her. He pulled her against his body, all warm and smooth, and kissed her with a force that stole her breath.

"I want to go slow, but I don't know if I can," he said harshly, and he parted her legs with his hand and found her hot and wet.

"We can do slow later...oh God, Joe." His fingers were busy and she'd lifted one leg, allowing him better access. But that threatened her balance as her knee wobbled, and she held on to his shoulders.

He swore again, and she smiled at the coarse words coming out of his mouth. She liked that he could be a bit dirty, and she whispered something in his ear that made him growl.

He slid his fingers out from inside her and cupped her bottom in his hands, then lifted her up so she was straddling him. There was a certain thrill in his strength, and he knelt on the blanket before laying her down.

He started at her breasts again, building her back up to a peak, then slid his tongue down the center of her belly before parting her knees. "Oh God. Joe. I..."

Whatever she had been going to say was lost as her hips jerked upward.

The climax built, but just as her muscles started to clench, he stopped, slid back up on the blanket, and kissed her.

She reached down and took him in her hand, the whole thick, hot length of him. He ground his hips, working with her, and then found her with his fingers again until they were mutually pleasuring each other, their breath harsh in the quiet space.

"I want you inside me," she breathed. "I don't have a condom. But I've been on the pill for years now." She felt the need to say it, hoping it didn't kill the moment.

"You're sure?"

"I'm positive."

He shifted again, parted her legs, and slowly slid inside her.

Oh. My. God.

"You feel so good."

"So do you. God, Cass, so do you."

They stopped speaking then, and only the sounds of pleasure drifted through the room. When she couldn't hold back anymore, she cried out and pulsed her hips against his. And as soon as she came, he flipped her over, gripped her hips, and took her from behind.

His fingers dug into her hips as he hit his peak. Cassidy collapsed, face down on the blanket. Joe, breathing heavily, dropped beside her. "Holy shit."

She chuckled, wonderfully languid and limp. "I can't move. I can't. It's physically impossible."

"Me either. Though at some point we're going to get cold. And we'll have to move."

"Nope. The fire'll keep us toasty." She turned her head to the side and looked at him. He was on his back, his eyes closed, his chest still rising and falling from the exertion. Yesterday he'd walked into the bank and watched her throw up in a garbage can. Last night he'd held her, pleasured her in a life-affirming sort of way. But tonight was different.

Tonight they'd met as equals, with equal wants and desires. And it had blown her mind.

"What are you thinking?" he asked. "I can feel you staring at me."

She laughed. "I'm just wondering how long it takes for you to be ready to go again."

He opened one eye, turned his head a bit, and grinned. "I'll let you know when I get feeling back in my legs."

She tried not to giggle; didn't quite succeed.

"Hey, Cass."

"Yeah?"

"I'm going to get a crick in my back if we don't move this somewhere else. Let's go get into bed."

Into bed. There was sex on a blanket but then there was sleeping together. Really, truly, spending the night. That was the part where feelings got involved. Was that what she wanted? Really? Or was this a weekend fling to let off some steam? This hardly seemed like the time to ask. Besides, there was only one bed. How could she say anything about sleeping together when it would mean him taking the couch...after what they'd just done together?

Besides, she really did want to sleep next to him. It just scared her a little. There was a big difference between being horny and opening yourself up to possibilities again. She hadn't really considered the reality of that before...it had all been theoretical. An if and not a when. Tonight she'd taken a big leap past "if."

He got up and held out his hand. She rolled over and took it, let him pull her to her feet. "Let me freshen up a bit first?" she asked, suddenly shy. Damn, their clothes were all over the living room.

As if sensing her misgivings, Joe came forward and cupped her face in his hands before kissing her softly. "This is not the time to start feeling bashful." He smiled against her mouth. "Go do what you need to do. I just want to feel you warm against me."

Why did he have to be so *nice*?

She spent a few minutes in the bathroom, and then came out again, still naked, since her bag was on the floor at the foot of the bed. Joe was lying on his side, and when she came out he flipped down the blankets. "Come on in. I warmed up your side."

She slid beneath the sheets, and her heart gave a little twist as he enveloped her in his arms. Damn, was he a cuddler, too?

They snuggled beneath the covers, their body heat gradually creating a cocoon of warmth while the soft cotton brushed against her skin. It had been a long time since she'd allowed herself the pleasure of sleeping naked. It had been a long time since she'd done anything like she had this weekend. Not that Joe needed to know that.

His breath was warm on her ear as he curled around her, spoon-style. "Hey, Cass?"

"Hmm?"

"You're sure the pill's okay? I just want you to know...well, there haven't been that many for me. Not really."

Interesting. "Oh?"

"My ex, and a couple of short relationships since. That's it."

She swallowed tightly. "For me either. None since the divorce, if we're being honest."

His hand rested on her hip. "Really?"

She nodded slightly. "I think this weekend is probably really out of character for us both."

"What do you suppose that means?"

Nothing she wanted to think about now. Just the idea made her lungs feel like they were shrinking, like she couldn't get enough air. It wasn't just about sex, or liking someone. It was her life in general. As much as she wanted to think she'd left her marriage behind, Darren was around all too often, reminding her of the mess. She'd decided to date again. Facing the reality of having actual emotions was something she hadn't prepared for.

"I don't know," she answered honestly. "I've kind of been enjoying the here and now. Everyone's allowed to do something crazy once in a while."

He chuckled. "If this is crazy, I wish I'd done it sooner."

She rolled over to face him. "Let's just deal with tomorrow when it comes, okay? I'd rather just think about tonight. And you and me and this bed. Let's hide away a little longer, Joe." She ran her fingers over his shoulder. "You did promise me slow, you know."

Even in the dark she could see the spark ignite in his eyes. "I did. And I try very, very hard to be a man of my word."

"That's what I like about you," she responded, moving into his touch.

Chapter Eight

T he sun was up by the time Cassidy came awake. Joe was still asleep, his dark hair on the pillow, the shadow of whiskers on his chin. She ran her fingers over her skin, wondering how many spots she might have that were raw from that stubble. She could think of at least three.

But it was Sunday. The secret weekend of bliss had to come to an end. She'd go back home. Probably have a meeting or something with a social worker or counselor. Hopefully, she'd go right back to work and give her manager a break after holding down the fort.

And Joe would go back to work, too. No one would know that when he was supposed to have been protecting her, they'd been having wild and crazy monkey sex.

She looked down at the bedspread. The sheets and comforter were twisted, maneuvered into a position that covered their bodies but definitely wasn't in the right place. It had been nearly three a.m. by the time they'd collapsed in an exhausted heap and pulled the covers up to ward off the chill. The fire had gone out long before their passion had been extinguished.

Cassidy slipped out of bed and tiptoed to the bathroom. It was cold, so she hurried to pee and brush her teeth, and then she darted to her bag and grabbed a pair of panties and a T-shirt. When she turned around, Joe was propped up on an elbow, watching her put them on with a look of satisfaction.

"Good morning." There was grit in his voice and it sent shivers over her skin. It was going to be harder than she thought to relegate this weekend to one-off status.

"Good morning yourself." Because she was freezing, she jumped back in bed and pulled up the blankets. "Fire went out."

"So it did."

"We slept late."

"We went to sleep late," he replied, raising an eyebrow.

"So we did."

She wondered if he was going to talk about what happened next, and curls of doubt and insecurity began to tangle down low in her stomach. But after a moment or two, he sighed, turned back the covers, and got out of bed.

What a glorious view.

He disappeared into the bathroom, and when he came back out, he'd slipped on a pair of sweats. He wasn't wearing a shirt, but that was remedied in short order as he grabbed a T-shirt from a drawer and pulled it on.

Then he sat on the bed and looked at her with a serious expression.

"I would imagine you'd like to have a shower. And I'll build the fire again." She was going to say something, but he shook his head. "Look, Cassidy. I think today you want things to go back to your normal life, and that's okay. I get it. You've been on a rollercoaster lately and normal probably sounds really good. So take a hot shower and I'll make us something to eat and we'll make this easy, okay? No regrets."

She did want to go back to her normal life...didn't she? It was a good life, after all. Maybe her ex was a bit of an asshat, but she had her independence, and a business she loved, and she had friends.

Except she *had* been looking for romance. And instead of finding it, it had found her. Boy, had it found her. Hit her like a ton of bricks.

She looked into Joe's eyes for a long moment. He could be very hard to read; was that his law enforcement training, or what? His eyes gave nothing away, and his face remained relaxed, his lips unsmiling but not frowning, either. Had romance found him, too? Or had it simply been a couple of nights of great sex? Scratching an itch? Heat crept into her cheeks. She would hate to assume, or make a fool of herself by thinking their time together constituted a relationship of any sort. Besides, all evidence to the contrary, she wasn't sure she was ready for anything that resembled an actual "relationship."

He'd said she probably wanted her life to go back to normal. Maybe he was the one who wanted it to go back to normal, and this was his gentle way of saying so.

"A shower sounds good," she said quietly, and tried a smile. "Thanks."

"There's no rush. Take your time."

Morning-after awkwardness. Great.

She went to her bag and took out a pair of jeans and an oversize sweater. "Don't worry about breakfast," she said, keeping her face down as she rummaged for socks. "I've got lots of food at my apartment. I'll be out of your hair in no time."

"You're not in my hair."

She grabbed the socks, turned around, and smiled brightly. "Oh, I probably am. You probably had other things planned for the weekend. Now that I'm not in any danger, you can get back to whatever."

She went to brush by him but he reached out and snagged her arm. "What's wrong?"

A frown puckered her forehead. "Nothing's wrong. I'm going to shower, that's all." He had gone from impassive to puzzled, so she reached for words to ease the situation. "If you want we can have breakfast at my place."

"You're in a rush to leave."

He almost sounded disappointed.

Cassidy looked down at her feet. "I'm just not used to doing this, okay?"

"This what?"

She bit down on her lip, glanced up, and then away again, toward the bathroom door and an escape from all the awkwardness. "This morning-after thing. I'm not sure what to say or how to exit gracefully."

His fingers eased on her arm. "You could start by looking at me."

Her gaze slid to his. Was it wrong that she wanted to forget the shower and pounce on him yet again? If it weren't so uncomfortable, it would be funny. Somewhere along the line she'd turned into a horny divorcée. Go figure.

"You are welcome to stay for breakfast. There's no rush to get you back to town. I'm not kicking you out, for Pete's sake."

He wasn't exactly asking her to stay, either. Or suggesting they see each other again. That was what made it so awkward. It was clear that this was a one-off. Not a one-night stand, but close.

"Sorry," she murmured, then tried to laugh a bit. "Don't mind me. I'm just being silly."

"Hey." He slid his fingers down her arm and clasped her hand. "It's fine. I'm glad that this isn't something you're used to." His smile was warm. "I'm not so good at navigating it myself."

She smiled a bit easier and held her clothes tightly against her chest. "And that's probably a good thing, right?" She shook her head. "You know what? I probably would have been horrible at the whole online dating thing."

"You're not going to reinstate your profile?"

"Nuh uh." She shook her head again and laughed a little. "I think Friday's little episode was enough excitement for me. Plus, I was honest, but clearly this guy wasn't. He didn't use his real name or anything. I just...I don't know. Maybe I'm old-fashioned."

Joe smiled down at her, his gaze dropping to her lips for a brief moment. "Oh, you're not that old-fashioned, Cass." Heat had just started to spread in her chest when he let go of her hand and backed away. "Now go shower so I can make us some coffee."

Cassidy escaped into the bathroom and closed the door, then leaned against it. Lord, she was an idiot. Why couldn't she just be cool and blasé about the whole thing? Oh no. She had to blush and stammer and look away because all of her bravado from last night had disappeared with the appearance of daylight and sobriety.

She turned on the shower and waited for the water to heat, then stepped under the spray and hastily scrubbed her body and washed her hair. Going home was definitely the right idea. She'd get her bag, go back to her own kitchen and bed and have internet access and, well, if not forget this ever happened, at least put it behind her.

Keep this weekend as a lovely memory from a really crap time.

It wasn't until she was dressed and back in the bedroom that she grabbed her phone and turned it on. It vibrated in her palm as it powered up, and then vibrated again and again as a flood of text messages came through.

One was from her manager at the restaurant; another from Sam at the station, with the same news he'd given Joe. The other fourteen were all from Darren, each one growing more insistent and angry at her lack of reply.

If this morning's awkwardness hadn't killed what little hope she'd had for romance, the text messages from her ex finished the job. She was far from being ready for anything serious.

Her apartment looked exactly the same, so she wasn't sure why it felt different.

Cassidy walked through the door and put her bag down by a kitchen chair. Her coffee cup and cereal bowl from Friday morning were still on the cupboard next to the sink; she'd been making up a grocery list over breakfast and the notepad and pen were on the small table, right where she'd left them. She'd been in such a hurry to pack her bag and get going that she hadn't touched a thing other than the necessities.

Nothing had changed at home. But she had changed. It had only been two short days, but she'd faced her own mortality, and that was a sobering thing. And then she'd been swept away to the other end of the spectrum. She'd never felt more alive than when she'd been in Joe's strong, capable arms.

"You okay?" His deep, warm voice sounded behind her, both comforting and stimulating. He made her feel safe, but oh, my. The soft tone rode along her nerve endings, making goose bumps shiver onto her skin.

"I'm okay." She turned around and smiled at him. "Thanks for bringing me home."

"Of course." He shifted his weight from foot to foot. "Is there anything I can do for you? Get you?"

She shook her head. "No, of course not. I'm fine. There's no threat anymore, and I'm snug as a bug here at home, right?" *Snug as a bug? Who the hell ever said that?* "I'll probably just return some phone calls and try to get a good night's sleep." Never mind that it wasn't even noon yet.

His smile lingered on his lips for an extra second, and heat crept up her neck and into her cheeks. They hadn't exactly slept a whole lot last night...or the night before.

"This doesn't have to be awkward," he said, reaching out and putting his hand on her arm.

But she disagreed. "Doesn't it? What would people say if they knew your protection detail included me spending the night in your bed?"

His cheeks turned ruddy now, and she wondered if she shouldn't have been so plain about it.

"Sorry. That was probably really blunt, huh."

He laughed a little and rubbed his hand over his face. "Maybe." The laughter faded and so did his smile. "The thing is, even if we did want to see each other again..."

Her heart lifted a bit, just knowing that he'd thought about it. She wasn't the kind of woman to have a fling and walk away without any residual feelings. It just wasn't her style. Right now she almost wished it was. Part of her wanted to see where this might lead. The other part was grounded in reality.

"It would look bad for you," she murmured, dropping her gaze. "I can see that. You're in a position of authority, and trust."

"I'm not above the rules, Cass. And I broke a lot of them this weekend. Besides, I would never want anyone to think I took advantage of..." He cleared his throat, and she looked back up at him. The desire to kiss the look of concern off his face was overwhelming.

"If anyone took advantage, it was me," she whispered. "Not you. I wish I could say I'm sorry, but honestly, I'm not. I know we can't carry on, but I'll remember this weekend for the rest of my life." Her statement sounded corny even to her ears, but it was the truth.

It was also fairly final.

"So will I," he replied. He looked over his shoulder at the door. He'd closed it behind him when they'd come in, and he reached back and flicked the deadbolt. "I know this is it. I just...damn, Cass. I just want one last kiss before I go."

"Me too," she answered, and lifted her arms so that her hands rested on his shoulders.

He put his hands on either side of her face, his fingertips stroking the crest of her cheeks as he leaned in. His lips were soft and seductive, with just the right amount of pressure, and she moaned a little as his tongue slipped inside her mouth. God, he was a good kisser. Demanding without being harsh, slow when it warranted, and with enough heat that her body tightened in anticipation. She ran her hands over his shoulders, then down over his shoulder blades and to the pockets of his jeans. Damn, but he had a fine ass.

"Cass," he murmured against her lips, and the single word sounded so desperate, so tender, that she pulled him closer, his zipper nestled between her hipbones.

He slid his hands beneath the hem of her sweater and pushed it up and over her head in one smooth, efficient motion. His fingers found the clasp of her bra and unhooked it, and both pieces of clothing dropped to the floor. Cassidy groaned as his palm cupped her breast. They shouldn't be doing this. They couldn't be together. And yet... they couldn't seem to get enough of each other, either. Want, desire, need...all those things ripped through her as she leaned her head back and Joe bent to her breast.

"One last time, and that's it." Her breath came in short gasps as his teeth scissored lightly at her nipple.

"Bedroom," he responded, and to her utter delight, he swept her up in his arms.

Chapter Nine

J oe traced a finger down the center of Cass's chest. She was so beautiful. He hadn't felt this way for a very, very long time. Being with her was more than satisfying a need; there was a connection he couldn't explain. Yes, right now it was very sexual. But when they were together, there was something more. A rightness to it that went far beyond physical attraction.

Right now she was stretched out on her bed, naked as a jaybird, looking lazy and well-loved. Her dark hair cascaded over the pillow and her eyes sparkled up at him. More than that, her nipples stood proudly and begged for more of his attention. She'd posed this way on purpose, he knew. And he liked her all the more for it. Friday night she'd been afraid, and in need of comfort. He'd been drawn to that side of her, but he liked this side more. There was a quiet, feminine power about her that was incredibly alluring.

"We've got to stop doing this," he said, frowning a little. His errant finger stopped just above her navel.

"We keep saying that. And then we can't keep our hands off each other." She rolled to her side a bit, and then slid her hand down between his legs. "See? I lasted what, five minutes?"

He choked on a laugh. "You're a very different woman today than you were on Friday."

She slid her hand off of him and rested it on his hip instead. Her gaze met his, and the teasing look was gone. "I keep going back and forth. It's an odd situation."

"It is."

"I keep asking myself what this is." She moved her finger back and forth between them, indicating that "this" was more like "us." "I keep telling myself that I'm involved more than you, but that's not true, is it?"

"I'm right there with you, Cass." His chest cramped as he admitted it. "At first I told myself that I was just helping you through a bad time. That you needed me. But last night..."

She nodded slightly, her eyes wide, and he felt himself slide deeper and deeper into complications. "Last night I threw caution to the wind," she admitted, and a little blush touched her cheeks. "And then this morning I had second thoughts. I was sure it was just a weekend thing for you and that you..."

He knew what she was getting at, and it scared him to death. But he wasn't a coward and he wasn't a liar, either. "You thought I didn't really care about you?"

She nodded.

"Of course I care. Hell. I've known you for a few years now. Since you were still married to Darren. I know you haven't had it easy. He was a real jerk when you guys split. You're not just some girl I picked up at a bar, okay? You're..."

Now it was his turn to pause. They weren't really friends, but they knew each other. They were acquaintances. Friendly. And this weekend they'd been *very* friendly. "You're different."

She sighed. "All you had to do was kiss me this afternoon and I was a goner. Joe, we do *this* really well." She waved her finger between them again. "But afterward, we're not sure what to do. And with your job, and the situation... It made me realize I'm not ready. For God's sake, my idiot ex texted me fourteen times over the last two days. I go back and forth between ripping your clothes off and being scared to death of what it means. I'm surprised you're not running in the other direction."

She was right, and they both knew it.

"You want us to back off," he said flatly.

"It's best for both of us."

He looked at her. Really looked at her. There wasn't an inch of her she could hide right now. The right thing to do would be to walk away. He let his gaze travel down her body, taking in the gentle curve of her neck, her pink-tipped breasts, the hollow where her waist met her hip, the long, smooth length of her leg. The entire problem was that he didn't want to walk away. He wanted to stay right here for as long as he could. In a capsule of privacy where they could make love until neither of them could think straight and they got this out of their systems.

The problem was he wasn't just Joe Lawson. He was Sheriff Joe Lawson and while what he'd done wasn't exactly wrong, it was a far cry from being right. If people knew what he'd done, his credibility would be toast. That credibility was all he had.

Damn.

Damn, damn, damn.

"You'd better go, Joe. Your truck's been parked outside for over an hour. Once word gets out that I'm home, anyone could come to the door. Or phone."

He frowned again. "Now I think I'm the one who doesn't know how to exit gracefully."

She smiled a little, and reached out and touched his lips with a finger. "Maybe there isn't a way," she said, giving a little shrug.

"I can't come back. You know that, right? I can't keep my hands off you, Cass. Now that I know... If we start carrying on, people will figure it out. I don't think I'm that good at a poker face. I'm the kind of guy who goes all in, you know?"

She laughed a little, ending on a sigh that reached in and wrapped clear around his heart. This was the right woman at the wrong time. Damn it again.

"You've actually got a pretty good poker face," she replied. "But I know what you mean. So...yeah. I understand, Joe. I really do. You're right."

They were on the same page, so why the hell was he feeling so damned disappointed? If she asked him to reconsider, he'd have to say no. Wouldn't he?

But she wasn't asking. She was agreeing with him.

He leaned in and kissed her, softer this time. It didn't matter. Soft and slow, hot and fast...her kisses produced the same result. They were close enough that the tips of her breasts touched his chest. He'd never considered himself a boob man before, but he couldn't seem to get enough of hers. The shape, the feel of them in his palm, on his tongue...

He needed to leave. And it needed to be a complete break. Anything else and they'd be falling into bed again. And again.

So he pulled back from the kiss, tucked a piece of hair behind her ear, and smiled. "Okay, then. I'm going to get ready to go."

She nodded.

As he got dressed, she got up from the bed and went into her walk-in closet. She came out a minute later, dressed in soft pajamas that covered her from ankle to neck. "I'm going to make tea and read and be kind to myself for the rest of the afternoon," she said, and he wanted to stay and serve her tea and watch TV while she read with her feet on his lap.

It wasn't just sex. He wanted her. He wanted to spend time with her, know more about her, be near her.

Shit.

Cassidy heard his truck leave and let out a breath. Unexpected tears stung the backs of her eyes and she blinked three or four times, trying to clear her blurred vision. This was ridiculous. It had only been three days. Not even three full days. They'd shared a few meals, a hike in the woods, and a bed. A weekend rendezvous. There was no reason whatsoever to be getting emotional about it. She'd been 100% honest when she'd said she wasn't ready. Just the thought of emotional intimacy made her stomach turn in a weird and unpleasant way.

She looked around her apartment kitchen and felt unbearably lonely. She needed sound. Movement. Anything to make her feel less isolated.

She put on the kettle and the soft hiss of water being heated broke the stillness. Food. She'd make herself something to eat. She opened the cupboards and went for the ingredients of her "emergency cake," then mixed them up in a mug and put it to cook in the microwave. Tea and cake. She'd feel better after that, right?

Then she went to the living room and turned on the TV. She'd Netflix something. Cake. Tea. Netflix.

Anything to stop thinking about Joe.

There was just one problem. She could still smell him—on her skin, her hair, in her memory.

She settled into a corner of her sofa and drank her tea, ate her hot cake, and stared at the TV without really seeing anything. Instead, her mind drifted to Friday's incident. God, she'd been scared. Not so much when it had been happening, because that had been simple reaction, but afterward, when she'd known she was okay. Joe had walked in and this great wave of relief had washed over her. Only then had the feelings rushed in, leaving her weak and wobbly.

He'd made her feel safe.

And then he'd made her feel cared for.

And in the end, he'd made her feel loved. Even if it was only for a few hours, she'd felt loved. That was something she hadn't felt in a long, long time. Since way before her divorce.

Maybe that was the problem. Maybe she was making way more of this than she ought to, because she'd been so hungry for affection.

"Yuck," she said aloud. Her last thought had sounded so needy in her head. She frowned at the screen, wondering why on earth she'd chosen *When Harry Met Sally*. She'd seen it tons of times already.

She might have thought about it more, but she heard a knock at the door and she got up to answer it. She checked through the peephole first, though. She was doing okay since Friday's robbery, but she was definitely more aware and cautious than usual.

It was her neighbor, Mary, from the apartment next door.

She pasted a smile on her face and opened the door. "Mary. How're you?"

"I'm just fine, dear." Mary lived with her retired husband and occasionally popped over with "extra" food, since she clearly didn't trust Cassidy to cook for herself, even though she owned The Forge. "I saw you got home all right. I wanted to stop in and see if there's anything you need. If you're doing okay." Her kind face was pulled into a worried frown.

I saw you got home all right. The apartments had shared walls, and Joe had been here a while. Heat flowed into her cheeks. Had Mary heard more than she'd bargained for?

"I'm doing just fine, Mary. It was a scary day, but now that the guy's behind bars, I'm just fine."

"I'm glad. Such a scary thing."

"It was. Do you want to come in?"

"Oh, I won't intrude. I'm sure you want to relax. But I wanted to bring you this." She held out a quilted carrier that Cassidy was sure held some sort of a casserole.

"You didn't need to do that. Thank you." She reached for the carrier and took it from Mary's hands. If her nose was accurate, it smelled like chicken pot pie. Way better than cake in a cup.

Cassidy put the casserole on the kitchen cupboard. "Are you sure you don't want to come in for tea?" Mary was undoubtedly looking for some details. Normally, the nosiness would bother Cassidy, but today her place seemed so quiet, she could use the company.

"Paul and I have dinner plans, or I would. There's a supper at the church tonight and we're going to the five o'clock sitting."

And so the casserole wasn't really an "I made extra and brought you one" thing. Mary had made it especially with Cassidy in mind. She was particularly touched.

"Well, thank you very much. I haven't really thought about cooking, and it smells amazing." On impulse, she stepped forward and gave Mary a quick hug. Her eyes stung once again. What the hell was wrong with her?

Mary patted her shoulder. "I just...well, you're all alone here, that's all. You need anything, you come knock on our door, okay?"

"I will."

Mary turned to leave, but only took a few steps before looking back at her. "Oh, and Cassidy? You could do worse than Sheriff Lawson." She winked and then headed back to her own unit.

Cassidy shut the door, certain now that her cheeks were flaming. Speculation after a simple weekend in "protective custody." Joe was right. They couldn't be seen together now without prompting comment. There'd likely be enough of that based on the weekend alone.

The last thing she wanted was to get him in any sort of trouble.

Chapter Ten

*O*ne month later...

Bubba's Pizza was running behind with their orders. Cassidy waited outside the strip-mall storefront, enjoying the last of the fall air. It was crisp enough now that she kept a scarf twined around her neck and thin gloves on her hands. The Friday Night Special included a pepperoni pizza and an order of wings. While Cassidy got a lot of her meals from the restaurant kitchen, some nights just called for extra cheese, deep fried chicken, and someone else to cook it. Tonight was one of those nights.

"Holding up the wall?"

She shivered at the sound of the voice, a delicious sort of ripple that she'd hoped would go away in time but aggravatingly hadn't. "Hey, Joe. Happy Friday."

He was in his uniform, including a puffy jacket and gloves, and his breath made little clouds in the air. She remembered how he'd looked the day of their hike in the woods. Not quite as official, but just as delectable. So much for putting that weekend behind her. Not that she hadn't tried.

"Friday's just another day." He shrugged. "I'm on shift this weekend. Thought I'd grab a slice before I head out again."

They'd said it was going to be a clean break, and it had been. She hadn't seen him since he'd dropped her off at home that Sunday. A different officer had delivered her subpoena, and a friendly lady from Boulder had called about counseling. She'd gone back to work as if nothing had happened. Joe hadn't brought any more dates into The Forge, either. In a town that was usually unbearably small, they seemed to have managed to stay out of each other's spheres of existence.

Until tonight.

"I've got tomorrow off," she said casually. "It's been a long week. I'm ready for some R&R."

"I hear you. Oh, guess what? I got a dog."

"You did?" Joe on his own was irresistible. Add a dog to that and, well, she'd be a total goner.

He nodded and grinned. It lit up his face and packed a wallop that hit her right in the chest. "Tim—you know, the other deputy?—he found a stray on the road and took him to the shelter. No one came to claim him, and he was a nice, friendly thing, so I adopted him."

Of course he did. Because Joe was the last of the really good guys.

"Don't tell me you got some little lap dog."

He shook his head. "Nope. He's a border collie cross. I keep trying to find things he can herd. He drives me crazy. And he loves squirrels."

She laughed. "I thought you were worried about leaving a dog at the cabin all day?"

He shrugged. "He seems to be managing okay, and sometimes I bring him with me." He wiggled his eyebrows. "My own personal K-9 unit." He leaned forward conspiratorially. "The girls in the office love him. Jessie's started keeping treats in her desk."

She'd missed him. More than she cared to admit. And she was both pleased and frustrated that he seemed so...happy, when she was just getting by day to day.

"Anything new with you?"

"Naw. Same old same old," she replied. "Work keeps me out of trouble. I just did the Friday deposit."

His expression sobered. "How has that been? Is it difficult going into the bank?"

It was. More than she'd expected. Going through the doors was no big deal, but each time she stood in line, she got a creepy-crawly feeling up her spine. As a result, she often turned at a ninety-degree angle and faced the door so no one was out of her field of vision.

"I manage. It'll get better."

Silence fell around them. Was he thinking about that day the way she was? For the most part, life had returned to normal, but she'd be a liar if she said she didn't still have the odd nightmare.

Finally she looked up. "No new blind dates?"

His gaze locked on hers. "No. None."

It shouldn't make her happy. It didn't, not really, but at the same time, there was something in her heart that rejoiced, knowing he'd perhaps been as miserable as she had. Still, if he'd changed his mind about seeing her, it wasn't like he didn't know where she lived. Or worked. He could have asked at any time.

He was still looking at her. "You?"

She shook her head. "No." It came out sounding a little bit strangled.

"Cass..."

"Don't," she said, her voice low. "I don't know how to do this. Let's just pretend we didn't see each other tonight."

"Is that what you really want?"

"Yes." No, but the truth was the intensity of her feelings, after two days together and a month apart, scared the hell out of her. As hard as she'd tried, nothing had been the same since that Friday when she'd first felt his lips on hers. She'd quickly become addicted, then quit him cold turkey. Now one conversation and she was craving his touch again. It was too intense, and she didn't trust it.

One of the teenagers that worked at Bubba's came outside, carrying a pizza box with a small paper bag resting on top. "Ms. Strong? Your order's up."

"Oh, thank you!" she was relieved for the out, and took the food from his hands. "Have a good night."

"You too, Ms. Strong." The boy's eyes widened and he gave a polite nod. "Sheriff."

She chuckled as the boy went back inside. "Well. You're impressively intimidating."

He reverted to his poker face again. "Really? I got the feeling I wasn't impressively anything. Goodnight, Cassidy."

He nodded to her and then turned on his heel. He hadn't even placed his order, she realized. For a moment she longed to call out to him, to tell him the truth. That nothing had changed.

But in the end, she stayed silent.

Because she was a chicken. Because her feelings hadn't gone away, and she wasn't sure what to do about it.

Could she really take a chance again? Was he even interested in anything beyond being friendly? Even if he was, she had a hard time believing that he'd stick around.

She went home and unlocked her door, balancing the pizza in her opposite hand. As she pushed the door open, she kicked an envelope that had been slipped beneath it. Frowning, she put the pizza down on the coffee table and went back to pick up the envelope.

It was from Darren; she recognized the handwriting on the front. For God's sake. Annoyed, she ripped it open and took out the piece of paper inside. As she scanned the letter, she wasn't sure whether to laugh or be angry.

He was making amends. Amends! Saying that he'd turned his life around and that he was sorry for all he'd done to make things difficult for her. For Pete's sake. Was he asking for forgiveness? She shook her head, marveling at his arrogance. She wasn't sure she'd forgiven him, exactly, but she'd made peace with the divorce. Darren was the past, and she never, ever wanted to go to that place again. It couldn't have been more over. Why would he think she'd care? His words were wasted—not that she believed them anyway. She didn't need him to make amends. She didn't need anything from him anymore. That in itself was a cause for celebration.

"Good for you," she said to the letter, then crumpled it into a ball and threw it into the recycle bin. He'd been the one to cheat and then piled the blame onto her. Most days she wished he'd simply dry up and blow away.

The letter, paired with the awkward meeting with Joe, left her feeling out of sorts. An hour ago she'd left work ready for a quiet Friday night and...happy. Now she was antsy and frustrated. She changed into pajamas, then grabbed a plate and a glass and put them on the coffee table. One more trip to the kitchen for a bottle of wine and a corkscrew and she was set for the evening.

A dozen chicken wings and two slices of pizza later, not to mention two glasses of wine, and she was having some regret. She was overly full and even more dissatisfied. How had she ended up this way, spending a Friday night alone? Maybe it was her fault, after all. Darren had called the shots for years and then he'd just...taken off with his younger, sluttier girlfriend. Left her high and dry. And Joe...well, Mr. Straight and Narrow had called it quits and not looked back. What was it about her that made her so leave-able? Why was she not enough?

She frowned and topped off her glass. She didn't mean that...not about Joe, anyway. He wasn't like Darren. He hadn't taken off with another woman. He hadn't asked for anything from her, as if she owed him anything. Still, there was this whole impropriety thing. He was so caught up in appearances and how things looked. He hadn't even tried to see her again. His silence told her he hadn't even been tempted.

You turned him away, the voice in her head reminded her.

"Shut up," she said out loud, and lifted her glass. She didn't need reminding. She'd been just as certain that he should go. Because she was afraid. Afraid of falling in love and being hurt all over again. Afraid that this time it would be more real...or worse, that it wouldn't, and she'd be repeating her mistakes.

It would have been nice if he'd found it just a bit difficult to walk away, though.

"Chicken shit," she said out loud again, though there wasn't a blessed soul to talk to. She burped and then took another long drink. How long was she going to play coward? Long enough to guarantee she'd always be alone?

Cassidy pushed her dirty plate piled with chicken bones to the side, then grabbed her laptop and booted it up. She clicked on the cowboy boot icon and up popped the Not My 1st Rodeo site. She hesitated for a moment. Maybe this was stupid. After all, look at what had happened already. But then she frowned. She'd told the truth in her profile. There were testimonials on the site, dammit. Happy endings. Just because one person lied...

And then there was the stark reminder that going it alone in this town was getting her nowhere. Why shouldn't she get out there and date? She drained the wine glass and filled it again, defiantly tipping up the bottle for the last drops. "I'm not leave-able," she stated to the empty room. "They're just leavers, that's all. It's not me. It's them. Jerks."

She clicked onto "My Account" and logged in. Her profile was disabled, and it took her a few confused minutes to figure out how to enable it again. When she did manage it, she let out a cheer, slopping a few drops of wine on her shirt. "There I am!" She toasted herself. "Cassidy Strong. That's right. I'm going shopping."

A rugged jawline and pair of blue eyes stared back at her.

"Well, hello, handsome."

She scrolled through several profiles, and her sips of wine got smaller and smaller. Eventually she got bored. This guy was too short. This one too far away. Another was clearly balding and his nose looked odd.

They weren't Joe. As she realized it, the wine soured in her mouth and she put the glass down on the table. Damn. That was it. They simply weren't Joe. They didn't have his smile, or that devilish gleam in their eyes, or the way he walked into a room and made everyone immediately feel safer. They didn't have his hands, and couldn't touch her like he could. Didn't have his lips or...or...

She pulled the throw blanket over her and fell back against the cushions of the sofa. When she closed her eyes, it felt as if the room was spinning, and she opened them again, trying to focus.

She was drunk. Drunk and sad and stupid. Stupid for letting him get to her this way. Stupid for not letting go.

Then she remembered something her mother had always said to her. "The heart wants what the heart wants." The words had always been accompanied by a weary shrug. Feelings were feelings. You couldn't really do anything about them, besides accept them and deal with them.

"I'll worry about it tomorrow," she mumbled, and burrowed into the blanket.

Chapter Eleven

J oe's shift ended at eleven. By the time he got to the cabin, it was nearly midnight. Flynn was barking up a storm as Joe shut the door of the truck. Cassidy had been right about that. It was nice to have him waiting at home. The house didn't seem so empty and quiet.

Of course it hadn't started feeling that way until after Cassidy had been there for the weekend.

For the first few days, he'd been able to smell her. The smell of her shampoo in the shower, that light, floral scent tangled up in the sheets so that every time he rolled over she was there again. Keeping away the last month had been hellish. He'd felt like one big walking hormone; distracted and, frankly, horny.

He'd thought he was past that. It had been nearly a month now since he'd walked out of her apartment. But all it had taken was one chance meeting and all the feelings came rushing back.

Never had he fallen for a woman like this. Not this fast, not this completely. He felt like a fool. She'd been cold and aloof earlier tonight. Clearly her feelings didn't match his.

He opened the door and waited for Flynn to rush outside to do his business. Once that was taken care of, he called the dog and they went inside. It was cold. The fire had burned out and so he left his jacket on as he built it back up again. Flynn circled madly around him, trying to jump up and lick his face.

At least somebody loved him.

His cell phone rang. What the hell...he'd been out of the office less than an hour, and already he was getting a call? He pulled it out of his pocket and looked at the number.

It was Cassidy. What the heck?

Heart pounding, he pressed the button on the phone. "Hello?""Joe? Zat you?"

"It's me. Cassidy, are you okay?"

"No, I's not okay, Joe. Know what?"

She'd been drinking. No doubt about that. He let out a relieved breath that it wasn't something worse, and sank down into the sofa cushions. "What, Cass?"

"Stupid site. All those guys...you know what their problem iz, Joe? Do you?"

He wasn't sure whether to laugh or sigh. She wasn't really making any sense, but he'd play along. He was tired and he was weak. He'd missed her. Even the current situation was better than nothing.

"What's their problem, Cass?" He said it quietly, and shut his eyes. Flynn hopped up on the sofa beside him and flopped down, resting his chin on Joe's thigh. Joe dropped his hand to rest on Flynn's warm back.

"They're not you, Joe. Joey. Joseph. Whatever Joe is short for. Anyway, not one of those guys is you and you know what that makes me, Joe?"

He was still trying to figure out who *those guys* were. "What does it make you?"

"Screwed. I'm screwed, Joe. And not in the good way. And it's all your fault. You and your...Joe-ness."

His heart surged. So maybe he'd completely misread the situation earlier. Maybe she did care.

"What do you want, Cass?" Nerves tangled in his stomach as he waited for her answer.

"I dunno." She sighed. "I don't want to be in love again. Love sucks."

"So this is a booty call?" Disappointment churned his insides. He'd already crossed a line when they'd made love—it had been vastly inappropriate in the situation. He wasn't going to compound that mistake by dropping by her house for a quickie. He wasn't sure what he wanted, either, but it wasn't that.

The line went quiet. "Cassidy?"

Nothing.

"Cass?"

There was a little click. Had she hung up? Put the phone down? He struggled to hear any background noise, but there was nothing.

All he could hear was her slurred voice saying, "They're not you, Joe."

He clicked off his phone and threw it onto the sofa cushion on the other side of the dog. Maybe she wasn't as cold as she'd seemed. Maybe...aw, hell. Truth was, she'd come along and hit him like a ton of bricks and he hadn't been the same since. Yes, it had been a crazy weekend of sex, but it had been more than that, too. There'd been talking, and going on the hike, and simply enjoying being together. There was his urge to comfort and protect her, to see her laugh, to pull her close and feel a calmness come over him as they snuggled together.

It hadn't been just physical. Sex was...well, sometimes it *was* just sex. But Joe wasn't a naïve kid. When it was with someone you really cared about, sex had the potential to be spectacular. It went past being bodies and became a deeper connection. He'd felt that with Cassidy. She was different.

And apparently so was he. He got a weird feeling in the pit of his stomach when he remembered the sound of her voice insisting, "They're not you, Joe." So what exactly were they doing apart, again? What was the worst that would happen if they started seeing each other? Gossip? Rumors? Would there be any protocol issues to deal with?

Their weekend together had been weeks ago. He still felt twinges of guilt when he thought about how he hadn't exactly done his duty...but why should he have to pay for that forever?

He thought about it for a long, long time; long after he should have been in bed catching some shut-eye. In the end he fell asleep on the sofa, with Flynn's warm body curled up next to his side.

—ele—

"Ow."

Cassidy peeled herself up from the sofa. The abrupt change of position was a mistake, however. Her head was pounding, a steady throb that brought to mind one of those wind-up monkeys with the cymbals, only with little hammers, banging on her skull from the inside.

"Son of a bitch."

Her glass of wine was still on the table, a third of it left. The smell alone was enough to make her stomach lurch. She picked up the bottle...it was empty. She never drank a whole bottle at one sitting. What on earth had she been thinking?

And then she remembered seeing Joe at Bubba's and she closed her eyes for a moment. The chance meeting had been more difficult than she'd expected.

Her laptop sat on the table, too, the cover not quite shut. She opened the lid and brought it back to life. The battery light was blinking, but there was enough juice to show her the last website she'd visited. Not My 1st Rodeo. She groaned. Had she really reinstated her profile last night? Oh, that shiraz had been full of false bravado, hadn't it?

Carefully as she could, she eased her way off the sofa and hobbled to the bathroom, where she peed, brushed her teeth, and put a cool cloth against her face. Then it was another slow trip to the kitchen for ibuprofen and orange juice. She wasn't sure what it was about the juice that appealed, whether it was the sugar or the vitamin C, but it tasted awesome on the way down. She prayed it stayed that way.

She was still in last night's pajamas and her hair looked like a bird had tried to build a nest in it. There were a few splotches of wine around the second and third buttons. She was still debating whether to shower first or try to eat something when there was a knock at the door.

Oh, God. And she looked like this. She could maybe not answer it...

The knocking came again, the sound like a drum against her head. She went to the door, wincing as it continued, and flung it open. "For all that is holy, please stop knocking!"

It was Joe. Looking showered and tidy and holding some sort of bag in his hands that smelled delicious. Which was something, considering the state of her stomach.

"Joe," she whispered, mortified.

"I'd ask how your head is, but I think you've already made that clear."

"What are you doing here?"

"I brought you breakfast." He lifted the bag. "The best thing for a hangover. Crispy bacon, scrambled eggs, and toast."

"There's bacon?" He was right about one thing. The odd time that she'd overindulged, the next morning she went for the OJ and the grease. It seemed to work miracles.

He laughed. "Oh, you sound very hopeful. Yes, there's bacon."

She opened the door wider. "I guess you'd better come in, then."

It wasn't until he was inside that she saw the hint of dark circles beneath his eyes. "Late night?"

"You could say that."

It was only nine o'clock. He was around early for someone who'd been up late. She frowned. "How did you know I was hung over?"

He hesitated, and she swore she saw a bit of pink beneath the slight stubble on his face. "Well...I guess you don't remember, huh?"

"Remember what?"

"You, ah..."

Suddenly she remembered something. Something she'd said, something about being screwed...

Embarrassment flooded through her. "Oh my God. I drunk dialed you, didn't I?"

He nodded. "You did."

"What did I say?"

He shook his head. "First, bacon. Then we talk. You need food. And coffee."

He shoved off his shoes and handed her the bags, then shrugged off his jacket and hung it over a chair in the little kitchen. Cassidy, thoroughly embarrassed and too out of sorts to have her wits about her, simply went to the counter and began opening the paper bags. One held a cardboard take-out tray with two coffees in it, plus little bottles of juice in the opposite corners to balance it out. The other had two foil containers with breakfast.

She peeled the cover off one. Fluffy eggs, four slices of crisp bacon, and four triangles of toast, which were slightly soggy now from the steam but would taste perfectly fine with some raspberry jam. She slid the other container across the counter and went to get knives, forks, and jam.

"You're not wasting any time," he commented, accepting the utensils. Cassidy didn't even bother going to the table. She was fine with eating standing up in this case. Fill the belly, then figure out what the hell she'd said on the phone. She was pretty sure it wasn't good.

Then again, he was here.

Which meant what she said might have been too good. Or at least too truthful. Oh damn...

She shoveled in a mouthful of eggs, stopped briefly to add pepper and salt, and then carried on. It took no time at all for her to finish the meal, saving one piece of bacon for last. She savored it, bit by bit, until it, too, was gone. Then she reached for the coffee and took a breath.

Joe was still only half-through.

"Okay," she said. "Spill. What did I say?"

He grinned. "You should be careful. You could give yourself indigestion."

She did feel the uncomfortable beginnings of a burp building. "I'm fine. Stop teasing me, Joe. I'm embarrassed enough."

"What happened last night?"

She sighed, frustrated. He was going to make her work for it. "After I saw you, I came home and had a letter from the ex. It made me mad, is all, and I had a little too much wine with my pizza and...yeah. So whatever I said, forget it."

"I find most people say things they otherwise might not say when they're drinking," Joe observed, spreading jam on his last triangle of toast. "Sometimes it doesn't make a lot of sense, and you have to put the pieces together. But it's usually truth that comes out."

What the hell had she said?

"Fine. Here's what I remember. I was mad. I was mad at Darren, and I was mad at you, and I went onto Not My 1st Rodeo and reinstated my profile."

"That's all you remember?"

She vaguely remembered scrolling through some of the profiles. And then...it was all fuzzy.

"That's it."

"Hmm." He munched the last bit of toast, then brushed off his fingers. She didn't even offer him a napkin. She was just so overwhelmed and feeling off-balance. "What did Dumbass Darren have to say?"

She couldn't help it; she laughed. "I've called him that in my head before. He didn't actually want anything. He left a letter. It was an apology. Who knows, maybe he's in one of those twelve-step programs or something." She rolled her eyes.

"What did you do with it?"

"Recycled it."

It was his turn to laugh.

But then silence fell around them.

Joe finally spoke. "What do you want, Cassidy? There's a reason why you went on the site last night, and a reason you called me."

"I was drunk."

"I call bullshit." Joe pushed his container to the side. "Seeing you yesterday was really hard for me, and I think it was hard for you, too. Let's finally be honest. Cass, I'm here because it's been a month and I can't stop thinking about you. I want to see you again. I want to see if what we have is—"

"Stop. Just...don't." What he was saying scared her to death. She'd fallen for Darren so hard and fast, and they'd been married before a year was out. But he hadn't been the man she thought he was. He'd grown distant, they'd stopped doing things together, and then he'd found someone younger and prettier to do them with.

"What are you afraid of?"

Everything, she wanted to answer, but she pressed her lips together and shook her head. She met his gaze. "You felt like you'd violated some sort of code for letting it happen in the first place. I don't want to be responsible for you losing your job or anything."

Joe rubbed his finger over his lower lip. "I see." He sighed and ran his hand over his hair. "I waited until now because you've been part of an ongoing investigation and court case. But now the guy's pleaded guilty. It's over, you know? Is it my job? Is it the fact that I'm a cop?"

She could take the easy way out and say yes. She knew his first wife had had a real issue with his profession, and all she had to say was yes and he'd leave, he'd stop making her examine all her insecurities.

He reached over and took her hand in his. "The truth," he reminded her.

"It's not your job."

"Why did you reinstate your profile on that site?"

Her head still ached; she pressed her hand to her forehead and closed her eyes. "I don't know."

"I think I do."

She dropped her hand and stared at him. "What do you mean?"

"You don't want something serious. You don't want anything where you might get in too deep. A dating site? You can go out on a few dates, decide they're not for you, and move on. Our weekend together suited you because after two days you could go back to your old life without any messy, complicated emotions. You're scared to death, and you've tricked yourself into thinking this is moving on."

She pushed back her chair and got up, rushing to the kitchen as harsh breaths filled her chest. She was angry and she was also so, so confused, because she suspected he was right. Had she really done that? Chosen an online dating site to avoid getting too close? Had she been lying to herself? If that were the case, then she really was screwed.

He got up and came to stand behind her. "Cass, maybe people will talk. Maybe I'll take some heat, and in the beginning it seemed like the cautious thing to do. But now...my feelings aren't going away. It's not the sex, though God knows, that was amazing. It's more than that. It's your laugh, and the way you look at me, and how we can walk through the forest and just talk and I can be myself."

"You're saying that the whole protocol thing isn't an issue for you?"

"It's one I'm willing to deal with, if it means being with you."

In that moment, a lot of things came clear for Cassidy. Despite her messy hair, wrinkled pajamas, and still-aching head, she felt a certainty that had been missing for a while now. It wasn't pain from a failed relationship holding her back. It was fear...pure and simple. She was terrified that she'd fall in love with Joe, only to find him falling out of it with her.

"I've been through a horrible divorce. I've felt...let down, and part of that is my own doing. I'm so afraid of being let down again. Of giving anyone the power to fail me...or make me feel I've failed them."

Silence fell in the kitchen. To cover the quiet, Cassidy began gathering the containers and cutlery and took them to the sink.

"Cassidy...what you're saying is that you don't trust me not to treat you badly." He frowned. "I'm not the kind of man who uses a woman."

"I didn't think Darren was, either."

"You can't compare me to him."

She spun to face him. "But I can have insecurities and fears and they're not irrational. I don't want to get burned again, Joe."

"So what? You're just going to date random guys from online dating sites to keep from being lonely, and never have a meaningful relationship again?"

"You haven't dated either."

"I've been waiting."

Fear rushed through her heart. "Don't say that."

"It's true. I was afraid, too. Afraid of what would happen if we were in the middle of the case and it was obvious that we'd had a fling. But this isn't a fling, Cass. It's more. At least it is for me. And last night, drunk or not, you pretty much said so, too."

She wanted to throw her arms around him and say none of it mattered, but then she looked around her tiny kitchen. This apartment, her frugal lifestyle, her own damned dog living at Darren's...it was all evidence to the contrary. It did matter. She wasn't sure she could take what little there was left of her and give it to someone else.

"You came over here with breakfast to profess your feelings?"

"Isn't it obvious? I can't get you out of my mind, Cassidy. Please, give us a chance. Let me love you."

She was getting close to giving in, but those last four words stopped her cold. Love...it was too much. Too scary, too heavy, too everything.

"I can't, Joe. I'm sorry. I really, really am." Even as she said it, she felt as if a hole was opening inside her, making an empty space that might never be filled.

His brow furrowed for a moment, and then he took one last drink of coffee and put the cup down on the counter. "Well. That's clear enough. I should probably be going. I'm on shift again this afternoon."

"Thanks for breakfast and for checking in with me." She walked him to the door and held it open. "And I'm sorry, Joe. You're a wonderful guy. You deserve someone who can give you everything, and I can't."

He turned and went to his SUV, and Cassidy took a step backward and shut the door. This was the right thing, wasn't it? Then why was she feeling like she'd just made a huge mistake?

Chapter Twelve

Thursdays tended to be busy at The Forge. Cassidy had happy hour specials that went from four until six, and most tables were full. Today's special was a pitcher of beer and a platter of nachos for fifteen dollars. The kitchen was handling things fine, but she found herself pouring pitchers from what was on tap at the bar. After six, the munchie crowd would thin and it would be back to regular dinner guests.

Still, she'd been on her feet since eleven, when they'd opened, stopping only briefly to inhale a sandwich mid-afternoon. Her hair was starting to come out of her braid a little bit, but she didn't have time to fix it. Maybe in a little while.

At least work had helped her keep her mind off of Joe for the past few days. It worked great until he walked through the doors at seven-fifteen, still in his uniform. The rush had calmed somewhat, but she still hadn't had time to fix her hair. She watched from behind the bar as he was shown to a table. Just the sight of him could still send her pulse racing. She wished it wasn't so. It had been four days of torture, of congratulating herself for being strong and then crying and berating herself for being foolish, scared, and stupid. Most of all, she'd done a lot of thinking about things he'd said. Especially one question.

You're just going to date random guys from online dating sites to keep from being lonely, and never have a meaningful relationship again?

She wasn't even thirty years old. At some point she was going to have to trust someone and let them in. She wanted to be happy. She wanted marriage and children and all the things she'd thought she was going to have when she'd said "I do."

Now he waltzed in here like nothing had ever happened, smiling at Kelsey, the hostess. It annoyed her. He should at least have the decency to look a little bit awkward and a lot less sexy. She couldn't think straight. All it took was one look at him and she started to turn to mush.

He took off his jacket, hung it on the back of his chair, and sat down. Then he looked up and saw her behind the bar and offered a small smile.

She could do this. It was business, after all. They were going to live in this town for a long time, and they were going to run into each other.

She filled a glass with iced water, grabbed a menu, and went to his table. "Joe." She put down the water and handed over the menu. "Just for one this evening? Or are you waiting for another blind date?"

Oh, why had she said that? She'd meant to be glib and casual, but it hadn't come out that way at all. She had sounded...snide.

"I'm waiting, actually. I'm hoping she'll join me shortly."

Oh. Her heart sank.

"Well, let me know if you need anything in the meantime. Would you like a drink of anything?"

He shook his head. "I'm still in uniform. Water's fine."

She went back to the kitchen. Her face was flaming and for some stupid reason tears pricked at her eyelids. She ripped the elastic out of her hair and started to rebuild her braid, her fingers ruthlessly efficient as she pulled on the strands. Just like that, he was on a date. Well, bully for him. She didn't need him. She didn't need anyone.

Needing wasn't the same as wanting, though, and that stopped her up every time.

"Hey, Cassidy? I think your phone is buzzing or something." Gilbert, one of the cooks, nodded toward her desk around the corner. "It sounds like it's vibrating up against something."

She thought about letting it be, but the distraction was welcome. "Thanks, Gil." The buzzing stopped when she picked it up, but the notification icon was on...and when she swiped her screen it showed activity at NMFR.

Interesting. She hit the link and was sent to her profile. At the bottom of the screen the cowboy hat was lit up—she had a hat tip from someone.

She touched the hat and a bubble popped up that said *Lawman32 has sent you a hat tip!*

Lawman32? She tapped the name and up popped the profile.

She nearly dropped the phone.

It was Joe.

Her office chair was only a few feet away, and she sank into it, her cheeks hot. He hadn't...but it was him. All dark hair and stormy eyes and luscious lips...

It showed his age as Summer—under forty—and that he was divorced. His likes and dislikes included walks in the woods, whiskey by the fire, and independent brunettes.

She bit down on her lip.

He'd set up a profile. And he'd found hers and made the first move.

Before she could think better of it, she hit the wink icon.

It was only thirty seconds and her phone buzzed in her hand again. This time it was a direct message.

Lawman32: *Hi FoodieGirl. Would you like to have dinner sometime? I know a great place.*

She choked on a laugh and messaged back.

FoodieGirl: *What on earth are you doing?*

Lawman32: *What does it look like? I'm wooing you.*

She pressed a hand to her heart. He really was. She got up and poked her head around the corner, sneaking a look through the kitchen to the dining room. He was sitting there, phone in one hand, holding his water glass in the other as he took a sip. She darted back into the office, her heart beating fast.

FoodieGirl: *What about what people will say? I hear you live in a small town where there's a lot of gossip.*

She waited.

Lawman32: *I'm not the kind of guy to let something like that keep me from being happy. I'm hoping you'll give me a chance to prove to you that I'm a good guy who won't leave at the first sign of trouble. What do you say? Start with dinner and see how it goes?*

Carrying on over text now was stupid. If he meant it, if he really meant it, she'd meet him half way. Her feelings for him weren't going away on their own. No one else measured up, and she was starting to think that no one else ever would. Everything she'd said to him about being afraid was true. But in acknowledging her vulnerabilities, she felt more empowered to fight them—instead of fighting her feelings for him.

She ran her hands down her shirt front, smoothing the fabric as best she could, and took a moment to freshen her lipstick and swipe a finger beneath her eyes in case she had any makeup smudges. Then she took a big breath, let it out, and stepped out of the kitchen.

He looked up. Their gazes caught, and so did her breath. He put down his phone, never breaking eye contact. By the time she reached his table, she could barely breathe.

"Sorry I'm late for dinner. I got caught up in the office answering some messages."

She slid into the chair opposite him. He held out his hand, palm up, resting it on the white tablecloth. The moment she put her fingers in his, he clasped them tightly.

"Don't apologize. Better late than never."

"Are you sure?"

His thumb rubbed against hers. "I'm sure. I'm really, really sure. We've got all the time in the world, Cass. I won't walk away if you won't."

She looked down at the napkin and cutlery on the table, blinking quickly. She hadn't expected this. Not in a million years. "But I sent you away..."

"And I listened to what you said—that you were afraid I'd give up and walk away. So I decided that I'd show you I won't. I'll be here, even when it's difficult. And maybe after a while you'll trust in me. In us."

She looked up, her lips open in surprise. "I don't know what to say."

His fingers squeezed tighter. "Say you'll give us a chance. One step at a time, right?"

"Right." She smiled, and something new lit up inside of her. Something she rather suspected was joy. "I'm not good at putting myself out there, but I'll try. I've thought about you constantly since that weekend, Joe. It was more than just..." She looked around to make sure no one was eavesdropping. "More than just sex for me, too. I felt a real connection, and that scared me. So I have to make a conscious decision to not let fear run my life anymore. Starting with this."

She got up from her chair and went to him, oblivious to whoever else was in the room, and did what she should have done Saturday morning. She kissed him on the lips. Not too long, but a sweet, soft kiss that sealed whatever deal they were making tonight.

"I've missed that," he murmured, as she took her seat again. "You know, we said one step at a time, but could I possibly suggest a first step right now?"

She had no idea what he was going to request, but she was pretty sure she'd say yes to just about anything. That kiss still hummed on her lips.

"What?"

"Can we please go in and delete our profiles on that website once and for all?"

Her smile widened as his chuckle warmed her heart. "Consider it done." She sent him a wink. "And I think we should skip dinner and get take-out. What do you say?"

He grinned back, and anticipation swirled through her belly.

"I say that's the best idea I've heard in weeks. But Cass?"

She was getting up from her chair when he said her name.

"Don't take too long, okay? It feels like I've been waiting for you forever."

She blew him a kiss. "And we have some time to make up for. But I'm ready to start if you are."

Turn the page to read the next Not My 1st Rodeo story, NOTHING LIKE A COWBOY!

NOTHING LIKE A COWBOY

Donna Alward

Chapter One

B rett Harrison stared at the computer screen in horror.

"Jesus, Manda. Are you crazy? You put me on a dating site?"

He stared at the picture of himself filling the top quarter of the monitor. It was a cropped shot from Manda's wedding last year, when he'd been dressed in a suit with a string tie and all the groomsmen had worn matching black Stetsons. It wasn't a bad picture, he supposed. But it did look like he was...well, posing for it, which made things worse. It made him look like he actually cared. Like he was serious about looking for love...when he hadn't even known the site even existed. And if he had known about the profile, he would have taken it down. Immediately. Like he was going to do right now.

If she weren't five months pregnant, he'd strangle his twin sister.

Manda perched on the side of the desk. "Hell yes, I put you on a dating site. It's time you got back out there. You're never going to get laid if you hole up in your office or in the barn or wherever."

He frowned. "My love life is none of your business."

"Right. And when you go around snapping at everyone? I want my kid to actually like his Uncle Brett. Trust me, big brother. What you need is a hot night of—"

"Of nothing," he interrupted, trying really hard not to be slightly amused. Trying to be mad. Ever since she'd gotten married, Manda had suddenly become an authority on romantic bliss. But to his mind, only desperate people used dating sites. The *facts* were just full of lies or inflated truths at best.

He wasn't that desperate. Was he? He wondered what Manda would say if he confessed that he hadn't been with a woman since his divorce. Or maybe Manda already suspected, and that was why she was pushing. Meddling.

"I can find a date if I want one." He scanned the rest of the profile and had to admit, Manda had been pretty honest. Of course, she'd only played up the good parts. He had faults. Lots of them. Sherry had been quick to point them out, too. It wasn't much wonder their marriage hadn't lasted, considering how little she'd thought of him.

Apparently, he wasn't romantic enough. Didn't tend to a woman's needs. Wasn't—and this was what stung the most—smart enough. Too rough around the edges. If he'd known she felt that way all along, they never would have made it down the aisle in the first place. And that wasn't an experience he was eager to repeat. It had very nearly cost him the ranch in the settlement. He wondered what his ex would say now that the situation had changed substantially. The ranch was in better shape than ever, and they were seriously looking at expansion.

Manda scoffed, giving him a slap upside the head to emphasize her point.

"Listen, you know as well as I do that offerings are pretty slim around here." He looked up at her. "Let's just take this thing down and forget all about it."

But Manda was stubborn, and she raised an eyebrow at him. "So which is it? You don't want a date or there's no one you like? Maybe you need to head into Gibson for a bit, hit the bar, whatever. Stop being so damned choosy."

"Manda." He was done fooling around, and he let his tone communicate that. "I don't want to be on a dating site. Take down the profile or I'll do it myself."

She grinned. "No. And you wouldn't know how anyway, because you're technologically challenged." Her expression turned smug. "Besides, you already have a date."

For five seconds, Brett was sure his head was going to blow off. "What do you mean, a date?"

Manda got off the corner of the desk and reached around him to slide the mouse over the mouse pad and click on an icon. "See? Melissa. Melly to her friends. You sent her a hat tip."

"A hat tip?"

"Well, yeah. The guys have to make the first move here, you know? See? She's checked off divorced, spring, and mutton busting." She straightened, crossing her arms with satisfaction.

"What the hell does that all mean? Manda, pregnant or not, you're walking a fine line here."

"It means" —she sighed with impatience— "that she's divorced, she's under thirty and she wasn't married very long."

He raised a dubious eyebrow and looked closer at the screen. For the love of Mike, the criteria the site used was downright hokey. His profile, on the other hand, listed him as divorced, summer because he was over thirty, and his marital experience as bull riding.

"Sounds great." Sarcasm dripped from his tongue.

"Yes, it does. Because you invited her for coffee."

He tamped down his absolute frustration at his sister's taking over the situation and replied through gritted teeth, "*I* didn't invite her anywhere."

"Well, I did for you. See? A coffee date. Very public place, limited time if need be, daytime. Women try to be really safe on first dates. She'll probably have a wingman ready to text her with an emergency if she needs an escape route."

It was sounding more like a military maneuver than a date. "What if I'm the one who needs an escape route?"

Manda grinned. "So you're going?"

"I didn't say that." He pinned her with his sternest glare. "Manda, you had no right to do this. To pretend to be me. To set this up. It's my life. I wish you'd respect that."

She stared right back. "I did it because I love you and I'm worried about you and I knew you wouldn't go do this for yourself."

"You're damn right—"

"And you've been licking your wounds ever since Sherry left. You need to get back out there, Brett. This girl doesn't have to be the one. But she might at least be a start to you realizing that not every woman out there views being a rancher as something that needs to be overcome. This site, it's specifically for people like you."

"People like me? What on earth does that mean?" There was actually a site for hermits? Desperate recluses? Eunuchs?

"Not My First Rodeo. It's for cowboys and ranchers, sweetie. And ones who've been around the matrimonial block and lived to tell the tale."

"And want to again, which I clearly don't. You forgot that part."

"You just think that." Manda frowned and put her hand on his shoulder. "Will you at least look at her profile? Buy her a cup of coffee? If you back out now, she's going to feel like crap."

"Then you can be the one to explain. I'm sure you'll let her down easy."

Manda's lips formed an ominous line. "Fine. Don't go. Whatever. Just stop moping around here and growling at everyone. We're sick of it."

She left the office, slammed the door, and silence fell in her wake.

Brett sighed, stared at the now-closed door and counted to ten. Why was it Manda always knew exactly what to say to get under his skin? Little sisters were the bane of his existence—and he had three of them. Manda, he took great pride in reminding her, was a whole seven minutes younger than him.

Hell, they were probably all in on this. Manda was the oldest and most often the spokesperson. Particularly now that she was pregnant with his first niece or nephew. Everyone knew he was a soft touch.

He turned in the chair and let his gaze fall on the monitor again. The screen showed the messaged conversation between himself and this woman. Melissa. Melly, he mentally corrected. Who the hell went by the name of Melly?

He clicked on her name, her profile popped up, and his mind went utterly blank for a few minutes.

He wasn't sure what he'd expected, but the woman on the screen was attractive. Really attractive. The picture was casual, looked like the background of house siding behind her, and she wore a simple blue plaid shirt, like she wasn't too worried about what she wore for the photo. Neither did she wear a lot of makeup, but she didn't need to. Her eyes were an intriguing almond shape and a soft, chocolaty brown, just a little darker than the smooth waterfall of hair that fell over her shoulder. A half smile touched her full lips. What on earth was a woman like that doing on a matchmaking site? Surely she didn't have any problem finding a date.

He went back to the message window and read what she'd written to Manda. Polite, modest, and claimed that she had never signed up for a dating site before. He wondered if that were true. Wondered if everything on her profile was true. It said she was twenty-nine, five-foot-nine and taught high school English. She was divorced and still hopeful there was a Mr. Right out there.

Well, wasn't that just sweet?

Brett pushed back his chair a bit and sighed again. Okay, so the photo had caught his attention. And the details weren't bad either.

But did he trust them?

No sir.

Still, his details were accurate. Maybe hers were too.

Hold on. Was he really considering going through with this farce of a date? He thought about what Manda had said. It wasn't this Melly's fault that Manda had impersonated him and set up a date. She'd be at the Daily Grind coffee shop tomorrow evening, waiting for him unless he told her otherwise. Standing her up was not an option. His mama had raised him better than that. And the idea of messaging her and calling it off...Manda was right. Canceling would probably make her feel like crap. It had to take a lot of guts to put up a profile and actually send someone a message.

He shook his head. What the hell was wrong with him? Why did he suddenly feel flattered that she'd said yes to a question he hadn't even asked?

He looked at the messages once more. "A cup of coffee sounds perfect," she'd answered. "I'm really looking forward to meeting you, Brett."

Aw, shit.

He was going to have to go through with it. But just one date. One coffee date. They could meet and be friendly and go their separate ways, and that would be that. And his profile was coming off the site as soon as it was over.

Damn straight.

Chapter Two

Melly stood outside the Daily Grind, her right hand gripping the strap of her handbag as she reconsidered for about the millionth time.

Why was she putting herself through this again? Was Brett already inside? What if he didn't show, like the last guy? What if he did but looked nothing like his picture? For a split second, she considered turning around and walking straight back to her car and heading back to Helena. Why had she ever thought that online dating would be a good idea?

But she wouldn't stand him up, because that would be rude. Besides, it was time she got back into the dating game. Sometimes she felt like she'd forgotten how to flirt. Banter. Have fun. Be herself. Fun Melly. Unfortunately, Fun Melly hadn't come out to play since signing up on NotMy1stRodeo.com. Her dates so far had been disasters.

One man had looked promising from afar, until he'd come closer and her nose had alerted her that he'd come right from the barn. There had still been manure on his boots, for God's sake. She was all for cowboys and ranchers but expected a man might clean his boots and change his shirt before meeting a woman for lunch.

Then there'd been the man who was at least fifteen years older than his picture and had only half the hair she'd expected. He'd been polite, but there definitely wasn't any spark. At all. The date had been painful and blessedly short. She'd felt relieved but also a little offended that he'd seemed to be in such a hurry to get away. And then, of course, the no-show. Wow.

She'd decided to throw in the towel, and then Brett had sent her a hat tip. She'd closed her eyes and sent a wink back to him before she could change her mind. The offer for coffee had come shortly after that. *One more try*, she'd thought. And when it didn't work out, maybe she'd let her BFF, Leanne, set her up with the gym teacher at her school. She'd been nagging Melly for ages about that—

"Melissa?"

She spun around at the sound of her name being spoken, her bag swinging with her, sliding off her shoulder and dropping to the crook of her elbow with a heavy thud. Yep, being herself sometimes translated into being a little klutzy and awkward. She scrambled to push the straps back over her shoulder while at the same time attempting a smile. Holy crap. She struggled to keep her composure, but her first thought was his picture didn't lie.

"You must be Brett. I'm Melly." It came out stronger than she expected, and she tried a smile with it, proud of herself. "Melissa. Melissa Walker."

The repetition of her name had probably wrecked any calm factor she'd achieved, hadn't it? She held out her right hand to shake his and *whoomp*. The bag slid off her shoulder again, jerking her hand downward. Her own damned fault for cramming it with her phone, wallet, emergency makeup and a hardback novel in case she ended up waiting...or worse. At least he hadn't stood her up. That was a good sign, right? She swallowed and held the smile, trying not to look like she was staring. Hells bells, Brett Harrison looked yummy enough to eat.

Once more, she shoved the handbag straps to her shoulder. "Sorry," she apologized, her cheeks hot, and he smiled in return. He had incredible blue eyes, she noticed. Nice and clear, with the tiniest of crow's feet in the corners and a fringe of light brown lashes. He hadn't worn his hat today, like he had in his profile picture, and she studied his hair, cut short around his ears, a little tousled on top, the same blondish brown as his lashes. The toffee-colored hair and blue of his eyes set off his tanned face, which she supposed came from working outdoors much of the time.

And his body... Well, it was impossible not to notice the tall, strong build. His stats had said he was thirty-two. Her heart gave a solid thump as she realized that Brett Harrison's profile had been one hundred percent accurate. He was exactly what she'd had in mind when she'd signed up on the dating site. A gentleman cowboy. And the way his sky-blue gaze settled on her now, a sexy one to boot. Maybe the other dud dates had been leading up to this. Who said persistence didn't pay?

Brett merely smiled at the awkward moment as she clung to her purse strap. "I have a mother and three sisters. I'm familiar with the phrase, 'my life is in my purse.'"

"It really is," she said, letting out a sigh of relief now that the initial introduction was over.

Brett gestured toward the door with a hand. "So, uh, how about we get that cup of coffee?"

She nodded, suddenly shy. Brett opened the door for her, and she scooted inside and then waited as he followed and they went to the counter to order their drinks.

"What'll you have?" she asked, determined to keep her chin high and confident, even though inside she was nervous as hell. The beginning had been less than auspicious, but there was time to turn it around. Be bright and sparkly. "My treat."

"I'll get the coffee," he said, reaching in his back pocket for his wallet. He was turned a little to the left and she got a passing glimpse of the square of his back pocket, a little more faded than the rest of his jeans. And resisted the sudden urge to fan herself.

Instead, she put her fingers on his arm, only briefly as she suddenly realized it probably seemed a little too familiar. "Brett, I'd like to buy you a coffee. Will you let me do that?"

James had been a stickler about paying for everything. He'd hated her trying to pay, like it was an insult, an assumption that he couldn't afford things, an affront to his masculinity. She really hadn't realized how much financial trouble he'd been in until he'd filed for bankruptcy. Anyone she dated had to get over that sort of male-pride thing. She figured this was a good first test.

He met her gaze for a long moment and then nodded. "I guess that'd be all right." He raised an eyebrow. "This once."

Meaning there'd be a next time?

"Good. Now what'll you have?"

He grinned. "A big mug of black. I'm a man of simple tastes."

She smiled back, encouraged. "You got it."

She ordered his coffee and then her own, which was slightly more complicated as there was a flavor shot and some steamed milk involved. But within a few minutes, they were headed to a table in the back corner of the shop that looked out over Gibson's Main Street. To her surprise and pleasure, Brett held her chair for her and waited for her to be seated before sitting across from her. Good looking—check. Manners—check. She wondered what else he had going for him?

"So," she said, laughing nervously. "Here we are."

"Here we are," he echoed, one corner of his mouth tipping up a little. He raised an eyebrow. "Let me guess. You're mentally going over my profile and trying to figure out if I lied."

Her cheeks heated again. "Clearly, you didn't." Rustling up her courage, she added, "If anything, the reality's better than the profile."

His laugh was low and warm and sent tingly feelings rushing through her body.

"I have to come clean," he confessed. "I didn't set up that profile. My sister did. I didn't even know about it until two days ago."

Disappointment flowed through her, and embarrassment. "Oh. I see. And she's the one who...?" Now she was feeling foolish. Naïve. "She sent the hat tip."

"Yes. I was really mad at her when I found out."

"I can imagine." Suddenly the coffee in front of her wasn't so appealing. Was he gracefully looking for a way to exit? He hadn't even asked her here today. His sister had. "You know, I was a little worried you were going to be a no-show."

He chuckled again. "I thought the same about you. And I thought about messaging you and canceling, but I realized it wasn't your fault my sister's an interfering pain in my butt. So I figured I'd show up, see if you did too, and have a cup of coffee. What could it hurt?"

This was sounding worse and worse. Like it was a pity date, for Pete's sake. She wondered how long she needed to sit here before she could get up and leave without being impolite. He hadn't wanted to be here. He was just showing good manners.

"Melly?"

She lifted her head and looked at him, surprised when he used the preferred shortened version of her name.

"You know, I'm not so mad at my sister anymore." And he smiled.

He had a good smile. The kind that made a girl feel like he was letting her in on some sort of secret. The kind that felt like it was for her and her alone. It was intimate, a little shy, a little bit cheeky. He rested his elbows on the table and it stretched the cotton of his shirt across his broad shoulders.

"You're glad you came?" she asked.

"More every second."

"Me too," she replied and smiled back at him. Okay, so less than a stellar beginning on both their parts...but it was showing potential. It was the smiling at each other that made everything seem suddenly, deliciously intimate. Something sizzled in the air between them. Was it too soon to be feeling any sort of attraction? And yet it was there, pulsing in the air around them, a tension that was as delicious as it was unnerving. Maybe she wouldn't need Leanne's help with that date after all.

He lifted his coffee cup and took a drink. She watched him, her gaze focused on his full lips as they touched the porcelain cup. Muscles tightened in familiar places. The words *dry spell* flitted through her mind, though she found she didn't care a whole lot.

Still. It was a first date. No sense in getting carried away. Much. She raised her mug and hid behind it for a few seconds, telling herself to get a grip.

"So," he said, sounding remarkably conversational. "You're an English teacher."

"Yes," she said, following his lead in the get-to-know-you portion of the date. "In Helena. I've been renting an apartment there since..." She swallowed tightly. The dating site was for second chances, after all. "Since my divorce."

"You seem too young to be divorced," Brett said, his brows pulling together. His gaze swept over her. "And far too pretty."

She absorbed the compliment and considered. How open should they be on a first date? What if there wasn't a second? She measured her answer. "I was young and a bit dazzled by him, I suppose. I met James when I was in college. He was charming and sophisticated and interesting. He liked nice restaurants and fast cars, and I guess I thought I did, too. At least for a while."

Huh. She hadn't really thought about it in that exact way, but the failure of their marriage hadn't been all James's fault. He'd lied and he'd hidden things from her, but she'd been pretending to be something she wasn't too.

"You don't like those things?"

"For a treat? Maybe. As a way of life? I'm not much into flash." She decided to keep the bankruptcy part to herself. No need to reveal everything all at once. "I'm a lot simpler, really. I'm a farm girl at heart. I realized I prefer big skies over bright lights. Food I can pronounce and identify over the latest fusion fad."

"You were raised on a farm?" Brett seemed both surprised and pleased by the knowledge.

She nodded and relaxed a little. She loved talking about home. "My parents have a small ranch about a half hour from here. I grew up growing my own vegetables and raising chickens, too." She grinned. "Actually, one of the things my ex-husband was most shocked at was that the eggs didn't come out all nice and clean and white like those from the grocery store."

She was gratified when Brett chuckled. She'd far rather talk about her upbringing than James. Especially now. Her dad's heart condition made it harder and harder for him to work, and he was set on selling the ranch, no matter how much she protested. It made her heart hurt just thinking about not having the place to call home anymore.

"How about you?" she asked. "Your profile says you're a rancher."

"Yes, ma'am. A beef ranch not far from here." He nodded. "You had a bit of a drive if you came from Helena," he acknowledged.

"Not that bad. I'm at the north edge of the city." She shrugged. "I'll probably stop at Mom and Dad's on the way home. Helena's close enough for me to visit lots. It's a nice day for a drive."

So it was. Late spring was beautiful in Montana. Everything turned newly green and lush, with clear blue skies and rolling farmland and jagged mountains. Melly loved her job, but this time of year, she always found herself missing all the spring activity. Right now, her mom would be putting in the vegetable garden. There was something so satisfying about putting seeds into the earth and being rewarded by green plants that would then become food. The closest she got to that was a couple of planters on her balcony. With a sinking heart, she realized this was probably the last garden her mom would put in at the ranch. Their plan was to move to a smaller house, on a smaller lot, closer to town.

It was bad enough that Melly's life had fallen apart. Why did the things she relied on to always be there have to change too?

"Busy time of year for you too," she said, taking another sip of coffee, determined to change the subject. She didn't need to kill the vibe with her depressing attitude.

"It's always busy," he replied, but he smiled again. "Though, yeah, this time of year is particularly hectic, and fun. A few weeks from now will be insane. Vaccines, branding, all the other necessary things that happen to new calves. I'm sure you're familiar with that."

She perked up. "Of course I am. Though I have to admit, branding isn't my favorite job." She sighed. "And it's not something I've been a part of much since college. I kind of miss it."

"You don't go home to help out?"

He couldn't know how hard that question was to answer. "Not as often as I'd like. Teaching is a pretty demanding job. Though I do visit more in the summer when I'm off." She didn't add that James hadn't liked the ranch. He hadn't liked the dirt or the smells or anything about it. She'd rarely gone home when they were together. It was only in the last year or so, since the divorce, that she'd visited more frequently, put on her boots, and gotten in the saddle again.

"It's probably the hardest time of the year," he admitted, "but I love it." He turned his coffee cup around in his hands. "Actually, I love just about every day on the ranch. I can't imagine doing anything else."

He looked up at her, and she could swear there was a defiant set to his jaw, as if daring her to challenge him. She wondered why. Wondered why he'd suddenly sounded a little defensive. If he expected her to disagree, he was going to be disappointed. To her mind, his life was pretty ideal. She was so done with the city, the cramped spaces and the traffic. Maybe it was true. You could take the girl out of the country, but it was a heck of a lot harder to take the country out of the girl.

"So," she said, a little nervous again, "you're divorced?"

"I am." He smiled grimly. "My ex-wife thought ranching sounded a lot more romantic than the reality."

Melly couldn't help it, she snorted. Brett's expression darkened.

She covered her mouth with a hand and tried to straighten her face. "I'm sorry," she offered, wanting to smooth the fretting wrinkle off his brow. "I didn't mean to do that. I shouldn't laugh."

"Yeah, well, I should have seen it coming. She never did really fit. I was just..."

"Dazzled?" Melly suggested, lifting an eyebrow.

His face relaxed a little and his eyes warmed, as if he appreciated the little bit of wit. "Yeah. Dazzled is one way of putting it. Thinking with the wrong head, if you'll pardon the crude expression."

She laughed again. And the wrinkle smoothed just a little bit more.

"Sounds like we both ended up with people a little flashier than our tastes," she observed. "Or maybe just a little too refined."

"Maybe," he conceded. "They might have done better with each other than the likes of us." He chuckled a little, and she got a whoopee kind of feeling from him pairing them together, even in such a casual way.

Melly looked down at her cup. Her coffee was gone. She suspected Brett's was as well. As dates went, it had been different. And since the word dazzled had been brought up more than once, Melly had to admit she wasn't quite seeing stars and rainbows. But then there was the hint of a smile he'd shown her earlier, and his manners, and that interesting moment where something had connected between them.

Not love at first sight. But intriguing? Yes. His foot bumped hers under the table and a zing went up her calf. Oh, definitely intriguing.

"Melissa?"

She met his gaze. His clear blue eyes were settled on her, his brows pulled together slightly as if he were trying to figure out a puzzle.

"If you don't mind me asking, why did you decide to use a dating site? You're a beautiful woman, and I can't imagine you being desperate or having a hard time finding a guy. I don't get it."

She pushed her cup to the side and folded her hands on the table, determined not to fidget or let her nervousness show. "Well, to be honest, I know what I'm looking for in a partner. I'm not a city girl, and I'm not new to marriage. I've always enjoyed the outdoors, loved growing up on our ranch. So I figured I'd narrow the search by parameters. The website helped me do that. Kind of a made-to-order thing." She let a grin crawl up her cheek. "You know, like Meg Ryan in "When Harry Met Sally". She orders things just the way she wants them. No compromising."

"And then has that I'll-have-what-she's-having moment."

Ah, yes. The orgasm scene. Melly met Brett's gaze. Was he flirting? It was hard to tell. He seemed more of a still-waters type than an open book. Still, it was a slightly suggestive comment to make at this point in the date, and she took it as a good sign. "You have to give the girl credit," Melly responded with a wink, flirting back. "She knew what satisfaction looked like."

The air hummed between them, and Melly lifted her chin a little, almost daring him to respond.

"Except she was faking." He raised an eyebrow and his eyes twinkled.

Game on. He was flirting with her. Melly felt a little more confidence slide through her and she leaned her elbows on the table, moving slightly more towards him, inviting him closer.

"Oh, she was just demonstrating a point. I've never seen the point in faking anything, have you?"

Two spots of color appeared on his cheeks. "Not really. I like a woman who knows how to speak her mind."

Was it getting warmer in here? It wasn't so much what they said, but the subtle undertones that seemed to raise her temperature. "Hey, there's nothing wrong with a little bit of mystery and surprise. As long as it's the right kind..."

The moment held, but then Brett suddenly leaned back a little, disengaging from the repartee. "Look, Melissa."

"Melly." She didn't like the sound of the way he said her name this time.

"Melly," he corrected. "Look, we're flirting a little here, and as nice as that is, I think I need to be honest with you, because I don't like to play games. You seem like a really nice woman. But you see...you're looking for something that I'm not. We don't want the same things, and I don't think it would be fair of me to let you think otherwise."

She appreciated his honesty at least. "Fair enough," she replied, surprised at how disappointed she felt. Just when they seemed to be getting somewhere, he backed off. "But I hope you realize that I'm not looking at each date as a first step to the altar. You seem like a good guy. Perhaps a little jaded, but hey, failed marriages have that effect. I went with the dating site because it seemed a little less, I don't know, meat-marketish than heading to the local honky-tonk for a few beers

and some dance-floor flirting. That's not my style. I'm more of a..."
But she couldn't come up with the right words. She was an English
teacher, and she was coming up blank.

Brett's smile blossomed. "More of an online shopper?"

She smiled back. "Wow, that doesn't sound much better, does it?"

They shared a chuckle and then he spoke again. "So you're actually
thinking you might find love this way."

"Well, yeah." It was her turn to frown. "I want to get married again.
Have a family. I figure meeting someone with common interests might
be a good start, you know?" She looked up at him and decided that if
he liked honesty, she might as well give him some. "That doesn't
mean I'm in a huge rush or that I'm taking inventory and trying to
check boxes. I'm open to dating for the fun of it." She blinked slowly.
"Do you get what I'm saying?"

"I think I do." His foot bumped hers under the table again.

"I'm glad neither of us chickened out today. Even if I do have your
sister to thank for it."

He grinned. "Busybody Manda? Yeah, I'm starting to forgive her
for her interference. I'm sorry if I'm a bit rusty. I haven't done this in a
while, and I was nervous as hell." Brett leaned forward on his arms,
just a little, like he was preparing to share a secret. "I have to admit I
was really relieved when I saw you."

"You were?"

"You seemed normal. And pretty. And like someone I might have
introduced myself to in a different situation. Then when your bag
kept slipping—"

"I know. I'm so awkward." Such an idiot.

"No, that's not it. I just...I used to feel out of place with my ex. But
when that happened, I don't know. It made me more comfortable. I
wasn't so intimidated."

The confession softened her heart just a bit. "Aw. And it makes me laugh to think of someone finding me intimidating. Most of the time, I feel like a square peg in a round hole."

He shook his head. "No way." To her surprise, his face went a bit red. "You're very pretty, Melly."

He'd called her pretty twice now, and it gave her a lot more confidence. "You're not so bad yourself."

And there it was again. That jolt of excitement, of anticipation. Startling by its very presence, and delicious too.

Damn.

She held out her hand again, this time without the handbag flopping on her wrist. "Can we start over? Hi, Brett. I'm Melly. I'm twenty-nine, divorced, and I like skies full of stars, long walks, a cold beer on a hot day, and wild roses."

He held her gaze as he fit his hand into hers. "Brett Harrison. I'm thirty-two, divorced, like the smell of fresh-cut hay, my mama's blueberry pie, watching the sunrise and" —he grinned— "a cold beer on a hot day."

His hand was warm, firm, lingering.

Then he squeezed her fingers in his.

"Do you want to get out of here? Go for one of those walks maybe?"

So the date wasn't over. Melly got the feeling that it was actually just beginning.

"I'd like that," she replied. "I think I'd like that a lot."

Chapter Three

They left the coffee shop and stepped into the bright May sunlight. Melly wasn't familiar with Gibson, though the town was small and easily navigated. When Brett explained that there was a walking trail a block and a half south of Main that went along the river, Melly thought it sounded lovely. And public.

The trail wasn't paved, but it was leveled and covered with a thin layer of finely crushed rock. They turned right, walking so the river was on their left, darts of light sparkling off the surface in the early evening sun. It truly was pretty, and Melly let out a breath, relaxing a bit more. They weren't the only ones out on the trail, and she was delighted to see the odd bench or picnic table set up for people to rest or enjoy the view. She imagined people coming here to have their lunch, or packing a picnic and letting their kids run free on the grass. "This is really gorgeous," she commented as they strolled.

"I'm kind of surprised you said yes," Brett replied, his boots crunching against the gravel. "My sister, Manda—the one who set us up—thought you'd probably bring a friend as backup. You know, meeting a stranger and all."

Melly looked up at him. "I considered asking my friend, Leanne, to come along. Honestly, I was glad you suggested coffee." She laughed a little. "Or rather, your sister did. Coffee is a low-maintenance date.

Easy escape route." She smiled. "Just in case you were a troll or creepy or something."

"And yet here you are out walking with me. Harder to escape."

"You're neither a troll nor creepy, so I don't feel threatened. Should I?"

He stopped, looked down at her. "No."

That little zing of attraction zipped between them again. Could Brett be threatening? *Maybe to my willpower*, she thought, unable to look away from his gaze. Earlier, he'd asked why she'd used a dating site. She wanted to ask him the same thing, because from where she was standing there wasn't a thing wrong with him. And, yes, she knew he hadn't actually been the one to set up his profile, but how did a guy like this stay single?

She struggled to keep things light. Breezy. "I suppose if you were some stalkery predator type, you'd hardly answer yes to that question."

He laughed a little, then feigned a serious expression and rubbed his chin. "That's true. You're taking a lot on faith here."

She turned away and sighed, the spell broken by the very suggestion of having faith in anything—or anyone. "I usually do. It's what got me in this position in the first place."

"Pollyanna syndrome?"

She was starting to see he had a subtle sense of humor that she enjoyed. "Maybe a bit. I don't get that vibe from you, though."

"I don't take a lot on faith," he admitted. "I like good solid evidence that I can see and touch."

Touch. Melly bit down on her lip as they resumed walking. She should not be thinking about him touching her, not this soon. They'd just met. But it wasn't difficult to let her imagination go there. He was a good-looking guy, rugged and capable and yet polite and funny. Then there was the shape of his lips that somehow begged to be kissed, the strong angle of his stubbled jaw that made her want to run her fingers along the side of his face. And he was just remote enough to make him a challenge. Not that she'd make the first move. Still, she'd have something to think about tonight when she was home alone.

"I understand that," she replied. "I find my optimistic outlook has a few more dark clouds than it used to."

"Divorce can do that," he agreed. "You know, it's not even so much the hurt anymore. I mean, I did love her. At least I thought I did, which at the time is the same thing. It's the damage left behind. It's the way you end up doubting yourself that really hangs on."

God, he was so right. She alternated between wondering how she could have been so blind to wondering how much of it was her fault. One minute she was strong and determined and had faith that there was love out there for her again, and the next she was terrified that she'd never be able to trust anyone, or take them at face value.

"Tell me about it," she answered. "I guess that's why I thought the site would be a good idea. I figured that if I dated anyone from there, they'd understand being gun-shy about the whole romance thing."

"But you said you wanted to get married again. That you believed in it." They skirted around a group of teens who crowded the walkway on their way towards town.

"Sure, in the grand scheme of things. Sometimes the practicality of it is quite different." She shrugged. "Maybe a few dates will at least, I don't know, get me out there again. Give me some confidence."

"Great. So I'm your guinea pig?"

His tone was teasing and she laughed. It felt really good. "How about...training wheels? I try to stay away from animal testing."

He laughed in return. "Training wheels. I don't know how to feel about that."

"Oh, don't worry. Hell, I haven't even..." She broke off, halting mid-sentence as her face flamed. Wow, had she gotten so comfortable that she'd been about to admit to her sexual dry spell, too? That she hadn't had sex in nearly two years? Twenty-seven. She'd been twenty-seven when the truth had hit. They'd been married for eighteen months. God, she'd been divorced longer than she'd been married. Twenty-nine was feeling much, much older than the number suggested.

She could feel Brett's eyes on her, and she struggled to breathe. "Well, that's embarrassing," she murmured, and she heard his soft laugh.

"If it makes you feel better, I haven't either. Not since Sherry left."

Sherry. That was her name. Then she absorbed what he was saying. They'd both been celibate since their splits. If anything did happen between them, they would be each other's firsts. She was kind of glad about that. Like she was at less of a disadvantage.

"Oh," she replied dumbly. The problem was, talking about the absence of sex in their lives had her picturing all sorts of things that she probably shouldn't be picturing on a first date.

They were getting further away from the main part of town now, the path meandering along the river bank to where a bridge crossed over, marking the end of the business district. The path passed beneath the bridge, and it was cool and shaded in the shadows. And private, she realized. They hadn't met anyone on the trail since the teenagers, and the kids were long gone.

Her heart pounded a little harder simply from the knowledge that they were alone. Had he brought her here on purpose? She felt about sixteen years old, sneaking away with a boyfriend to find some secluded corner to make out. And God help her, she loved it. It was exciting. It made her feel vibrant and alive again. And maybe just a little bit adventurous since Brett was virtually a stranger.

"Melissa."

She didn't bother correcting him. Her name sounded different on his lips this time, like a caress, and his voice was dark and soft as it echoed off the concrete.

"Yes?" She turned to face him, and her heart leapt even more at the serious expression on his face.

He reached out and took her handbag from her shoulder and placed it on the ground by her feet. "Maybe we should just get this out of the way."

"M...my bag?"

He shook his head, stepped closer so that their bodies were nearly brushing and she could hardly breathe.

"Kissing," he said, the timbre of his voice deeply intimate.

She didn't want to stammer. Wanted to be flirty and confident and seductive, but that had never been her style. "Oh. Well, I suppose it would be a good litmus test, you know, to see if we're compatible and all and..."

She was babbling. And she stopped abruptly when he put a finger gently against her lips.

In the next moment, he was kissing her. Or almost kissing her. It was hard to tell, because she could barely feel his lips on hers. But they were there, fluttering, teasing, inviting rather than possessing. Their breath mingled and her eyes fluttered closed as she simply enjoyed the anticipation of what might come next. One thing for certain—Brett Harrison knew how to take his time and make a woman long for more. Because when he opened his lips and deepened the kiss, she forgot all about this being a first date and looped her arm around his neck, pulling him closer.

He was a good four or five inches taller than she was, and when his arm came around her, he pulled her up so that she was on her toes. His tongue swept in to taste hers. His tasted of rich coffee and man and dark desire. It exploded between them, and before she could sort out any kind of rational thought, he'd lifted her off her feet and cupped her buttocks as she instinctively wrapped her legs around him. A half a dozen steps and her back touched something cold and hard—the concrete of the buttress.

This was crazy. Insane. But there was no denying that the chemistry she'd sensed earlier was definitely there between them. His hips pressed against hers and she felt a carnal longing so intense it took her breath away. "Mmm," she murmured into his mouth, and when he slid his wide hand over the pebbled tip of her breast, the sound was replaced by a gasp of pleasure.

Brett let her down slowly, put his forehead against hers and shifted slightly, putting a little space between them. He was breathing hard, and she matched him breath for breath.

"Holy shit," he said, inhaling deeply. "Holy shit."

Melly's voice was shaky. "Well. There was nothing awkward about that."

"Maybe we should have broken the ice that way. Saved ourselves a lot of time." She felt his face shift slightly as he smiled.

"It would have caused quite a scene on Main Street," she reminded him, her back still against the concrete, her body still humming from the stunning assault on her senses.

Brett stood back, and she knew she flushed again when he adjusted his jeans. "I didn't intend for all that to happen," he said, apology in his voice. "I thought I'd kiss you. Without an audience. See if there was any chemistry."

"Test the waters."

"Yeah. I didn't expect to... Well, I don't think chemistry is a problem." He let out a low, sexy chuckle.

Melly gathered up all the confidence she could muster. "I'm not sorry you did," she said plainly. "Bit sorry you stopped, though."

His eyes held hers for a few moments, as if he were asking her to clarify what she'd meant. Would she have gone further? Would she have slept with him on a first date? Not here, not under a bridge like a horny teenager. But she wasn't sure she'd have stopped him from going further, either. And if he asked her to follow him to a hotel right now, she'd be tempted. Mighty tempted. If the heat of that kiss was any indication, sex with Brett was guaranteed to be hot.

The problem with hot was that it was far too easy to get singed.

"I should probably walk you back to your car," he suggested, and she couldn't help feeling a little disappointed. Maybe he didn't want it to go further. Or maybe he was simply being a gentleman. What a novel idea.

"Okay," she answered dully.

"Mel…" He reached for her hand. "It's the first date. I don't want to rush things, that's all."

She felt a sliver of relief, knowing that he simply didn't want to move too fast. Back in the spring sunlight, they reverted to polite chat about Gibson, her job, the ranch. Nothing flirty, nothing suggestive. But Melly's lips still hummed from his kiss, and the little knot of tension low in her belly refused to go away.

Before long, she was pointing at which car was hers and their steps were slowing on the sidewalk.

"Well, here we are," she said lamely. She pasted on a smile and looked up at him, feeling increasingly awkward. Boy, it was hard getting back into the dating game again. Other than the few minutes when her hormones had taken over, she'd second-guessed just about everything today.

"Here we are," he echoed, his voice deliciously deep. Melly wanted to see him again. She knew that for sure. But she didn't want to be the one to ask. Despite putting herself on the website, she still liked the guy to make the first move.

"Thanks for the coffee," she said, then bit her lip. She'd bought the coffee. Man, he had her rattled. "I mean..."

"I know what you mean," he answered. Her bag was starting to slip again, and he reached out, adjusted the strap so it was on her shoulder, his fingers brushing her arm. Goosebumps rose up on her skin at the contact, and nerves tangled in her belly as he stepped closer.

"I had a nice time," he said softly, and then he dipped his head just a little and kissed her lightly. Just a soft, brief graze on the lips, but it was enough to nearly put her into meltdown.

"Me too," she said on a breath, blinking and looking up at him with dazed eyes.

"If you're interested, I'd like to see you again." Brett reached around her and opened her car door.

"I'm interested," Melly said quickly, and then figured she looked overeager. She wondered if the day would come where she wouldn't feel like an idiot.

"Should I just message you through the site?" His blue eyes rested on her, and her nerves were so ramped up now that it felt like her whole body was on alert.

"Do you have a phone?"

He reached into his back pocket and took out his cell. She took it and quickly entered her number. "Here. Now you can text me. Or call. Or...whatever."

"I'll do that. Maybe we can go to dinner or something."

"That sounds good." She smiled. Wondered why on earth she thought grabbing him by the shirt collar and dragging him into her backseat sounded more preferable to a dinner date.

"I'll be in touch then." He smiled. "Thanks for the coffee, Melly."

"Anytime," she replied, and got into her car while he was still holding the door. He shut it behind her and then moved to the sidewalk, lifting a hand in farewell as she pulled away from the curb.

"Well," she breathed, looking at him in her rear-view mirror. "I'll be damned.

Chapter Four

Brett wasn't about to tell his sisters a thing about his date, other than she was nice and it went well. When Manda pressed him about whether or not he was going to see Melissa again, he merely shrugged and said he wasn't sure. But he placated his sister by asking her to give him the password for his profile, which she took as a good sign that he was on board.

And then he immediately changed the password so she couldn't get access anymore.

He texted Melly and asked her to dinner on Friday night, saying he'd drive into Helena this time. They agreed that she'd make reservations for eight o'clock since she knew the city restaurants better than he did, and she'd meet him there. Brett was nervous as hell. Melly was looking for love. He wasn't. She was open to dating for fun...that he could handle. Dinner was easy, but what about after?

There was no denying there was chemistry, but how far did he want things to go? What was, well, appropriate? Shit, he hated dating and rules and just...everything. He was still kind of reeling from the first date, if he were being honest. He'd gone to be polite and ended up beneath Memorial Bridge with her legs wrapped around him. Lord, she'd been sweet. Sweet and sultry.

At a meeting with his lawyer on Wednesday, he was so distracted that he barely registered that his latest offer on a property had been turned down. He finally turned to his buddy Austin for advice. Austin was married with a sweet wife and a little boy, but he was still good for a few beers and lots of laughs. Austin clapped him on the back, congratulated him on getting back out there again and handed him a box of condoms. Now, Brett was standing in his room, dressed in jeans, boots and a sport coat, hoping he looked okay. He stared at the box of condoms on the bed. It would be presumptuous to think that they'd sleep together on the second date, wouldn't it? On the other hand, things had gotten pretty hot the other day. Wouldn't he be smarter to be prepared? She didn't need to know he had them with him. He wouldn't want her to think he was expecting anything...but if the opportunity did present itself...

Cursing, he opened the box, ripped one off the strip and tucked it into his wallet. Damn, just thinking about it had given him a hard-on. He ripped off another one and put it with the other. A guy just didn't know. He'd rather be safe than sorry.

They'd made arrangements to meet at the restaurant, and Brett used his phone to find the location and parked his truck in a nearby parking garage. He was surprised to find the restaurant was so small, but his mouth watered when he stepped inside. The smells were fantastic. It wasn't anything flashy or extravagant, but the warm colors in the decor and the candlelight made it cozy and welcoming. Sitting at a table for two was Melly, her dark hair falling over her shoulders and a glass of white wine in front of her. She looked up at him and suddenly her eyes lit up and she smiled.

"Do you have a reservation, sir?"

He dragged his gaze away from Melly and focused on the hostess. "My date's already here, thank you."

"Of course. Can we bring you a drink to start?"

He couldn't care less, but he nodded anyway. "I'll have whatever she's having," he suggested. Without waiting, he made his way past the other diners to reach their table.

Melly stood up as he approached, and his eyes goggled at the sight of her. She was wearing a dress, and she had fantastic legs. The dress itself wasn't especially fancy, but the draped style highlighted her curves.

"Brett," she said, and her smile lit up her face.

The anxiety he'd suffered the whole drive to the city dissipated as he met her beside the table and kissed her cheek. "I'm sorry I'm late."

"You're not. I was a little early." Her cheeks colored prettily. "I don't know why, but while I was waiting, I was afraid you weren't going to show or something. I feel better now."

Their waitress brought a glass of wine and put it on the table in front of him. He started to laugh. "Excuse me, but could I have a whiskey, neat please?"

"You didn't order the wine?"

"I did. It's just..." He smiled at her, feeling a little bit foolish. "You can leave it, too. Thanks."

As the perplexed waitress left, he looked at Melly, who was watching him with confusion. "It's your fault," he said. "I saw you sitting there and the hostess was asking if I wanted anything and all I could think of was, 'I'll have what she's having'."

When she laughed, the sound was enchanting. "Do you realize you've used that line in both of our dates?"

Right. The "When Harry Met Sally" thing. "I guess I have." He shrugged. "What can I say? You look beautiful, Melly."

"Thank you. You look pretty good yourself."

"I had help."

He probably shouldn't have admitted that, but it slipped out. After their coffee date, he'd also wondered what had compelled him to be so honest with someone he'd just met. God, he'd even talked about Sherry, which he never did. Maybe it was because Melly didn't seem to have an artificial bone in her body. She was incredibly genuine, or at least she appeared to be. And it prompted a comfort level that surprised him.

"You did? Your sister again?"

"Hardly. I'd rather keep her out of my business. A friend of mine. Who has a wife. I made sure she confirmed his advice for what to wear."

She laughed lightly. "They sound like nice friends."

"They are," he agreed. "The best." He and Austin had been in some good scrapes together. Brett had three sisters. Austin was the closest thing he had to a brother.

The waitress returned with his whiskey and menus, and for a few minutes, they pondered what to order.

"What's good?" he asked. "I'm guessing you've been here before?"

She nodded. "Only a few times. My favorite is the gnocchi, but you might want something more...meaty. I've had the thyme chicken. It's lovely."

He went with the chicken, because he had the sudden idea that eating anything with linguini or any type of long pasta could get messy. After they ordered, bread came, followed by a house salad. By the time the entrees were delivered, his whiskey was gone, Melly had accepted the second glass of wine and they were chatting easily about work.

It was easy. Almost too easy, Brett realized. In between bites, Melly told funny stories about her high school students and the pros and cons of teaching that particular age group, which led to sharing a few tales of their own teenage years. They ordered coffee and Melly suggested dessert to share, and they agreed upon the dark chocolate roulade. Her eyes had lit up when she saw the dessert menu, and the decadent choice didn't disappoint. Watching her put the spoon in her mouth and close her eyes with appreciation made his brain shift forward to the next part of the date...if there was, indeed, a next part.

He wanted there to be.

Brett put down his spoon, no longer hungry, and fixed his gaze on her face. There was something about her that drew him in. Maybe it was the way she smiled, or the softness in her eyes that put him at ease. And he was certain that she had no idea of the innate sexiness she possessed. There was a grace to the way she moved, a certain something that caught a man's eye and kept it.

"I'm so full," she announced, licking the last of the chocolate off the spoon. "I made a complete pig of myself and I can't find it in me to be sorry."

Several comments rushed through Brett's mind—about licking the spoon, about needing her energy for later—but he didn't say them. Instead, he reached across the table and took her hand in his, twining their fingers together.

She looked surprised, and then a little bit pleased as she held his gaze.

"What would you like to do now?" he asked, rubbing his thumb over the top of her hand.

"Oh. Well..." She hesitated and then smiled. "What would you like to do, Brett?"

He measured his words. He was quite good at self-editing when he put his mind to it. "For starters, I'd like to kiss you again."

Something flickered in her dark eyes. Desire? Awareness? Whatever it was, he liked it.

"Brett," she said, her voice low.

"You asked," he reminded her, smiling a little. "But whatever comes next is up to you. If you want me to take you home and call it a night, that's okay. It's been great spending the evening with you." In his head, he knew there was a benefit to taking things slowly. It didn't mean he necessarily wanted to.

"A drive home would be fine," she answered, and he tried to quell the disappointment he felt at the simple words. Maybe Manda had been right. Maybe he had been licking his wounds for too long. It was possible it was past time he got back into the dating world again.

Melly gripped her clutch purse tightly as they made their way out of the restaurant into the spring evening. Brett took her hand as they walked to the parking garage, and she thought about his last words. He wanted to kiss her again—for starters. What else did he have in mind? Did she want the same thing?

He opened the door to his truck and she hopped in, tucking her skirt around her legs and fastening her seatbelt. They were going back to her place. And she'd have to decide whether to leave him at the door or invite him in. She knew what she wanted. She just didn't know if it was the smart move.

Brett eased the truck out of the garage and back on to the street. With the radio playing softly in the background, she gave him directions, and soon they were heading north. It would only take a few minutes to reach her apartment. Minutes that seemed to go by so fast and yet so slowly.

"Take a left at the next set of lights," she instructed softly, her hands fidgeting in her lap. Brett was not interested in a serious relationship. She knew that. She was looking for something permanent...eventually. But maybe not yet. She'd done a crap load of thinking over the course of the week and she'd realized it wasn't fair to pin a prospective-husband tag on someone after a date, or even two. Why couldn't they just be in the moment and see where it led? Didn't that make more sense?

"Turn right, and it's the second building on the right," she advised. As he turned the truck into the small lot, she pointed at a few vacant spaces. "That's visitor parking."

He pulled into the spot and put the truck in park, then killed the engine. When she would have reached for the door handle, he put his hand on her left arm.

"Wait," he said, his voice a low rumble. "I'll get it."

With her stomach in knots, Melly waited as Brett hopped out and went around the hood of the truck to open her door. He held out his hand and she took it. She got out gingerly and reached back for her clutch.

"No big handbag tonight, huh?"

"Not tonight," she said, a little bit breathless as she faced forward again and found herself close to his broad chest.

They started walking to the door of the building, and Melly's nervousness ratcheted up several notches. Should she say goodnight at the door? Invite him in? If she did, would he make assumptions? Damn it, wasn't dating supposed to be fun? Instead, she felt as though she were walking through a field of landmines, afraid to take a step unless it was a mistake.

Brett stopped at the main door and waited. She was glad. He wasn't assuming anything and that helped. "Thank you for dinner," she murmured and then ran her tongue over her lips that suddenly seemed dry.

"It was nice," he replied and put his hand on her wrist, squeezing lightly. "And nice to spend time with you again."

She looked up. The tension sizzled between them, the elemental attraction that she simply couldn't deny existed. Was it so wrong to want to enjoy it? Maybe the whole narrow-down-the-search thing had been a good idea at the time, but right now she didn't want to think too far into the future. She wanted to enjoy the here and now. And right here, right now, Brett Harrison was standing in front of her, his fingers circling her wrist, his lips slightly parted and his eyes locked on hers, waiting for her to make the next move.

"Nice is an innocuous word," she said softly. "It was a good date, Brett. And I don't think I want it to be over yet. Do you want to come up for a nightcap?" He smiled a little and she winced on the inside. Could she have said anything more cliché? It sounded like something a woman would say on one of the soap operas she used to watch after school...

"I'm driving, so a nightcap might not be the best idea."

Disappointment and embarrassment rushed through her.

"But I'd like to come up anyway."

Whoosh. There went the embarrassment and back came the nerves. The excited thrill-of-the-unknown kind. "Right. Let me get my key."

She dug in her purse and got her key, and after she unlocked the door, Brett held it open, letting her through. They did the same at the inner security door and then she led the way to the stairs. "No elevator," she explained quietly. "But I'm only on the third floor."

Their shoes made scuffing noises on the industrial-grade carpet that covered the hall and stair steps. There wasn't another sound in the building as they made their way to her apartment door. Her hand shook as she put the key in the lock and the door swung open.

She reached for a light switch while Brett closed the door behind them.

"Nice place," he said quietly, and she took a deep, steadying breath.

"Thanks. Come on in." There, that sounded calm, didn't it? Her heels clicked on the ceramic tile of the entry as she put her purse down on a small table. "It's not very big, but there's just me."

She put on a smile and turned around. But the moment she did, the awareness seemed to overflow. Alone. Her apartment. Just the two of them. Before she could register a coherent thought, they each took a step towards each other. Brett's strong arms came around her and lifted her to her toes while she cupped his face with her hands and kissed him.

There was no easing into this one. It was pure, unadulterated desire that pulsed between them. "I waited all night to do that," she said on a soft breath, stepping back and gripping the lapels of his jacket. She pushed it off his shoulders and tossed it at a chair so that it draped there, lopsided. Her busy fingers fumbled at the buttons of his shirt while he simply pulled on the tie at the waist of her dress and it fell away, the wrap-style now gaping in the middle.

"I love that this is easy access," he replied, his voice rich and dark. She was still working on the buttons of his shirt when he put his hand over hers and stopped her progress.

"This is what you want?" he asked, his blue eyes piercing hers. "You're sure?"

There was a moment of uncertainty and she paused. "You don't?"

"Oh, I do," he confirmed. "But you need to be sure. We won't do anything you don't want to."

She could see the hollow of his throat, a V-shaped slice of skin visible where she'd unbuttoned his shirt. She wanted to taste it, to touch it. She wanted to feel strong and sexy and not awkward and unsure. For some reason, Brett was able to make her feel that way. He had from the moment of the first combustible kiss.

"I'm sure."

"Then, darlin', take that off for me." There was so much heat in his voice, she could swear her uterus contracted in simple anticipation.

"The dress?"

He nodded, slowly. "The dress. But you might want to leave those shoes on."

Melly swallowed. If that wasn't the sexiest thing she'd heard in a long, long time... She hoped her hands steadied as she found the fabric of her dress and eased it off her shoulders, letting the silky material puddle on the floor at her feet.

She was incredibly thankful that she'd had the foresight to wear good underwear. Her bikini panties were pale pink, with swatches of lace over the hips, and the bra matched, the plunge accentuating her cleavage. The look of bald admiration on Brett's face told her he approved.

"Your turn," she instructed.

Brett lifted first one foot and then the other, taking off his boots. Then he pulled the tails of his shirt out of his jeans and her mouth went dry as he undid the rest of the buttons, revealing a tantalizing glimpse of his chest and abs. God, he was sexy. Did he realize it? She didn't think so. There wasn't a trace of smugness on his face. Just longing—and intent.

"Come here," he said, and she took the few steps necessary to stand in front of him. She put her hands inside his shirt and touched the hard warmth of his skin, loving when a muscle ticked in his jaw. Daring, she kissed the center of his chest, then slid her mouth over to flick her tongue over a small nipple, smiling when he swore under his breath.

She put her hands at his waist, unbuckled his belt by feel alone and slid the button from the hole so that only the zip remained fastened. To her delight, Brett shrugged out of his shirt and hauled her close, the heat of his skin soft and warm against hers as they twined together.

They kissed right there at the spot where the tile entry met the soft carpet of her living room. A little squeak came from her mouth as he picked her up and carried her to the sofa. He put her down gently and then lowered himself on top of her, his strong arms braced on either side of her head and the stiff fabric of his jeans pressed against her panties. She wrapped her leg around his hip and arched up, rubbing against him as their kisses grew more fevered. He slid down a little and bit at her nipple through her bra, and she cried out as pleasure darted through her body.

Despite the urgency, Brett took his time until she was hot, pliant, and so ready she thought she might lose her mind. He reached back into his pocket for his wallet and she saw him take out a foil packet before dropping the wallet on the floor.

She sat up a little, put out her hand when he would have returned to the sofa. "Not here," she said, her breath coming fast and hot. "Follow me."

She took his hand and led him to her room, stopping only to click on a bedside lamp, giving the room a soft, warm glow. It had been so long since she'd had sex, so long since she'd felt this carnal and beautiful. She wanted to see him. And she wanted him to see her. She helped him take off his jeans, stripped off her panties and then nudged him down on to the bed, taking the condom from his hand and putting it on him herself.

"Mel," he murmured.

When she lowered herself onto him, his head went back, his eyes closed, and she hesitated a moment to enjoy the sensation of him inside her. But soon the urge to move took over and she started a slow rocking that picked up pace as his hands gripped her hips.

"You feel so good." She sighed, bracing her hands on his pecs. "So good."

"God...you...too." His icy-blue gaze was on her, and he bit down on his lip when she gave her hips a sharp thrust. "God, woman..."

Crazy, that was what this was. Crazy and awesome, and she let all of her inhibitions go. She bent one knee up towards his ribs, straightened the other and levered her hips, feeling the orgasm building inside. Her hands were on the pillow on either side of his head, and as she moved he caught the tip of one breast in his mouth.

That was all it took to light the fuse. Two thrusts later, her world came apart, her body shuddering over his as she cried out.

She was vaguely aware of hearing her name as Brett put one strong hand on her bottom and met her thrust for thrust. They were a tangle of limbs and sweat and sex as they came down from their climaxes, their breath harsh and satisfied in the quiet of the bedroom.

Melly shifted, he slid out of her, and she collapsed beside him on the bed.

"Whoa," he said, a low sound of awe that made her feel sexy and accomplished and inordinately pleased with herself.

"Mmm," she replied. The cool air in the room caused little goose bumps to erupt on her damp skin.

"I need to...uh..."

She chuckled into the pillow. "Bathroom's the door on the right," she said. Funny how now that the moment was over, he was bashful. But then that was part of what she liked about him. He came across like this quiet guy, all manners and still waters, but then there was this intensity about him that hinted at the fire beneath the surface.

And so far, she'd touched the flame and hadn't been burned. She smiled to herself as he walked to the door, and she admired the rear view.

He was back moments later, his hair tousled, his skin flushed. Melly remained lying on her side on the bed, her elbow under her head, still catching her breath. Brett reached for his boxers and slipped them on before joining her on top of the bedspread.

He assumed a similar pose, propping up his head on his hand and he smiled at her. "Okay?" he asked.

"Very okay," she replied, moving her foot and sliding her toe along the side of his calf. "I don't know what it is with us. It's like we touch each other and...well, it's like lighting a match."

"I know. I hope you're not asking me to be sorry. I still feel like I'm having a slight out-of-body experience."

She laughed. "Me too. That was good, Brett. Really good."

"I don't usually move this fast. I mean, second date and all. Pretty sure my mama would flay me alive."

"You're a bit old to be worried about your mama," Melly laughed.

"Are you kidding? Obviously you haven't met mine." But he was grinning. "Seriously though. I'd be given a lecture on respecting a woman and taking my time." He frowned. "I'm not sure what I'm trying to say here, except this kind of thing isn't something I make a habit of."

Clearly, if it was true that he hadn't been with anyone since his divorce. Her heart melted a little bit at his consideration.

"I wasn't exactly taking my time either, cowboy." She ran her fingers over his ribs. "I knew the first time you kissed me that if it came to this, it would be good. Thanks for more than living up to the expectation."

His eyes glowed at her. "Damn, I like you."

"I like you, too."

There was another decision to be made, and that was where to go from here. Invite him to stay? The idea of waking up with him was enticing, but it might also be too soon. So far, it had been two dates and one major release of pent-up sexual energy. Yet she didn't want him to just get up and get dressed and leave.

"You want to stay a while? We could, you know, talk or something."

"Or something?"

"Don't you need recovery time?"

He laughed then, a big, full laugh that warmed her down to her toes. She couldn't help but join in. Damn, this whole thing was surreal. Just a week ago, she'd been scared he'd be a no-show at the coffee shop. It had been slightly awkward, until he'd kissed her. That had been different. That had felt right from the start. Just like tonight.

Maybe their relationship was going to be based on sex. If that were the case, it would burn out soon enough. The idea was slightly depressing, and her laugh drifted away.

"What do you want to talk about?" he asked. And then he rolled to his back and stretched out his arm, inviting her to curl into his side.

Melly got off the bed, went to a chest at the foot and took out a soft blanket. She spread it out and then got under it and covered them both as she cuddled into his body. Mercy, he felt good. All heat and muscle and lean strength.

"How about you tell me what you've been up to?"

"Just the regular ranch work. It's not that interesting. Besides, you probably have some school stories that are more entertaining."

"A few that would curl your hair." She chuckled. "You know, I love teaching literature. And this can be such a great age. But oh my God, the hormones. The drama."

He chuckled. "I remember my sisters at that age."

"Oh, it's not just the girls." She turned her head and looked up at him. "Boys are almost as bad." She grinned. "Almost."

She sighed. "But you know, sometimes I envy them. At that age, the world is your oyster. There are no limits, only ambitions and dreams."

"And you've given up on dreams?"

"I don't know." She pursed her lips, considering. "It's not even that. It's more...I don't know. The world changes. Things that you count on that disappear."

He shifted his weight a little. "You mean your marriage?"

She supposed she did, in a way. But lately, she'd been thinking more and more about her mom and dad. They'd been her one constant through everything. Home was always home. The idea of the ranch not being a place to go home to anymore...

If only her cousin Dustin could get approval from the bank, at least it would stay in the family. But this week her mom had confessed that they'd had an offer and they were tempted.

"Mel?"

She liked how he called her Mel, not Melissa or Melly. It was like the shortened version of her name was only for him. Once more, she sighed, feeling weary. "It's my mom and dad's place. Dad's heart won't let him work it anymore, and to be honest, they can't afford to keep it. It's up for sale. And I know they've had an offer and it makes me sad."

"Of course it does. It's your home."

"Yeah. It's kind of...well, it's not just a house. It's a whole way of life, constant and secure. Only it's not. That freak storm last year? It cost Dad a quarter of the herd. Between that and his illness... But I thought it would always be there for me to go home to."

She was mortified to find her eyes had watered and her voice wobbled.

"I'm sorry."

"No, I'm sorry. I didn't mean to get emotional on you." She lifted her hand and scrubbed her eyes. "Honestly, I'm kind of mad. I don't even know who at. Circumstance, maybe. Shit, Melly Carmichael is supposed to be tougher than this."

Brett's hand had been stroking her arm, but suddenly he stilled. "Did you say Carmichael? I thought your last name was Walker."

"Walker's my married name. I never changed it back."

"And your parents live where again?"

A little bit of unease trickled through her. "Just east of Lincoln."

"Christ." Brett shifted, sat up a bit. "Not Jim and Becky Carmichael?"

She pushed herself up on the bed, clutching the edge of the blanket to her chest. "Wait. You know my parents?"

"We've met. Mel, I'm the one who put in a bid on the ranch."

She stared at him. "You? But..." God. Little things started racing through her brain. Was it all a coincidence? That out of all the girls on the dating site, he'd picked her? That he'd just happened to mention a purchase over coffee last week? She knew for a fact that her parents had turned down his offers. Three of them, to be exact, but they were weakening. He wanted the property, and he wanted it badly. The question was how far was he willing to go to get it?

Enough to use her? She scrambled off the bed, snatching the blanket and wrapping it around herself, leaving him exposed. "You need to go."

"Mel." He had the audacity to look surprised. "Look, I had no idea..."

"Really? You really didn't?" She lifted her eyebrow in a cynical arch. "Was this all part of your plan? What was the idea, get me talking and find out if my parents were softening or what it would take to get them to say yes? I'll answer that right now. Never. You are *never* going to buy our ranch."

Forget the nerve to be surprised, he was actually angry if the thin slash of his lips and furrowed brow were anything to go by.

"What exactly are you accusing me of? Sleeping with you to... what? I didn't even know who you were."

"So you say." She was naked under the blanket. *Naked.* She thought she might actually be sick. "My *sister* set up my profile. My *sister* contacted you first." She shook her head as she mimicked him. "You really expect me to believe that?"

"It's the truth. A dating site is not my speed at all. And I only agreed to meet to be polite."

Ouch. Why that actually hurt her feelings was a mystery. "Well, what a gentleman you are. You wine and dine me and get me in bed with you and during the day you're working to destroy the one thing that still matters to me."

Brett reached for his jeans and pulled them on. He shoved the rivet through the hole and glared at her. "This had nothing to do with you. It's business. I want to expand our operations and the ranch is perfect for us. I didn't even know you existed. I'm not trying to take advantage of anyone here." He rammed his shirt tails into his jeans and zipped them up. "Least of all your parents. The price I offered your folks was more than fair. More than."

"Well, aren't you just a paragon of virtue."

"You're angry," he said, straightening his shoulders. "I get it. You don't want them to sell the place. But they are going to sell it, Melly. So maybe you should take some time to decide who you're angry with. Because I don't think it's me. It's them. Or yourself. Or whatever."

She couldn't think of a single thing to say.

"I'll see myself out."

He left her standing there in the bedroom, and she heard the door shut behind him.

Chapter Five

B rett was still angry days later. Even the grueling branding weekend hadn't eased the knot in his chest.

He ran the brush over Charley's hide, putting lots of energy into it. The old horse loved every stroke and closed his eyes lazily, his skin shuddering from time to time. Brett sighed and dropped his forehead to Charley's smooth neck, just for a moment.

"Women," he breathed, then straightened and rolled his shoulders. "You're smart to steer clear, Chuck." Charley's eyes stayed closed, but he flickered his ears at the sound of Brett's voice. "I didn't even want to go on that date. And then I ended up liking her. Damn, I liked her a lot. And then she hit me right in my pride."

Charley's lashes fluttered. Brett gave another long stroke of the brush.

"I mean, I understand her being surprised. And even upset. But she insulted my character. My ethics. My manhood."

"What about your manhood?"

Manda was standing at the stall door, one shoulder resting on the frame.

His sister was not the person he wanted to see right now. "This is all your fault," he said, pointing the brush at her. "So don't bat your eyes like you're innocent and give me that wounded-girl look. That hasn't worked since we were kids."

No batting of eyes. She raised one eyebrow. "What the hell did I do now?"

"You set me up on that website, that's what." He tossed the brush into a bucket. "Of all the gin joints in all the towns in all the world..."

"What are you muttering about?"

"Melissa, that's what." He gave Charley an absent pat, picked up the bucket and headed out of the stall, passing his pregnant sister with as much indignation as he could muster. He hated that he had a soft spot where she was concerned. "Shut the door."

"What about Melissa? I thought you went out again."

He wheeled on her as she was latching the door. "The ranch I bid on? Turns out it's her parents'. And she's pissed."

Manda's eyes widened. "That's a crazy coincidence."

"Yeah. Except she doesn't think it is a coincidence. She thinks I engineered the whole thing."

"That hardly seems likely." Manda frowned.

"That's what I said." And he realized that Melissa had spoken in the heat of the moment. But it had been over a week now, and there hadn't been one single text, let alone a phone call.

It wasn't just the accusation he couldn't forget. It was the hurt look in her eyes. That he even had the power to hurt her was surprising. They hadn't known each other that long. Long enough to sleep together, he reminded himself.

"So what's the status on the bid now?" Manda's question brought him back to the present.

"There was a counteroffer. I'm upping my bid."

"How long before you top out?"

His smile felt grim. "I can't go any higher," he said. "I've thought about just letting it go. But that's hardly logical, is it? I mean, someone's going to buy the place if I don't. And it's perfect for what I want."

Manda came over and put her hand on his arm. "I'm sorry, Brett. If you don't get it, there'll be another place to go up for sale that's nearby."

"I know. It's just a pretty piece of land. And with Mom and Dad and you guys sticking around here..."

"I know. You want your own place. To make your own mark."

"To expand Lazy H. There's a difference."

"Maybe your loyalty to this place is how Melissa feels about her folks' place, too."

"I've thought of that. I'm not blind or stupid. But I didn't date her with an ulterior motive. Hell, you're the one who set us up."

"And if I'd known who she was, I never would have suggested it."

For all Manda's manipulations, he believed her. Because he had faith in her. Something that had been completely lacking between himself and Mel.

Then again, they'd gone on exactly two dates. How was she supposed to have faith in someone she barely knew? Chemistry, desire...that was one thing. But trust was something entirely different.

"Brett, maybe you need to talk to her again. If you argued, you both probably needed time to cool off."

"If she's cooled off and hasn't been in touch, doesn't that mean she still thinks I used her?"

Manda let out a huge sigh. "Maybe she's waiting for you to cool off and deny it. Maybe she thinks your silence indicates guilt. Until this misunderstanding, did you like each other?"

Heat crept up his neck and he turned away and walked towards the feed room to get Charley a scoop of oats. "We got along okay."

Okay, hell. Maybe he'd be less offended if he could get the picture of her on top of him out of his head for five minutes.

"Then maybe you shouldn't give up so quick."

"Manda, two dates isn't really a huge emotional investment. I'll get over it."

"Great. Then we should browse the site again—"

"No." He held up his hand. "Just no." He scooped up some oats and started back to the stall. Anything to keep his hands busy. Keep moving. Because if Manda took one look at his face, she'd figure a whole lot of stuff out. She'd always been able to read him like a book, and it drove him crazy. Having a twin was sometimes awesome but sometimes a big ol' pain in his ass.

"Well, you've turned into Crabby McCrabby Pants. Maybe you should just talk to her, instead of leaving things the way they are."

"She has my number."

Manda smacked herself in the forehead. "Will you forget your pride for two seconds? Men."

"Women," he responded. But then he couldn't help it. He smirked. And she smirked back. "All right. I'll call her or something. At least clear the air. Calmly."

"And what about the ranch?"

He shrugged. "It's exactly what I'm looking for to complement our operation, but my budget isn't limitless. I've got one more chance, but if the other party counters, I'm out."

And wouldn't that make Melissa happy. Except someone else would still be buying the property. She had to realize that the problem wouldn't go away even if he were out of the picture.

It took him two more days to work up the nerve to send her a simple text that said, *"Can we talk?"* And a day after that for her to reply with a blunt, *"About what?"*

He waited until work was done for the day and his parents were inside watching the evening news. Part of the reason he was excited about the prospect of expansion was the chance to get out on his own again. Since the divorce, he'd stayed at his childhood home while his house had sold, and the proceeds split between himself and Sherry. It was time. A man his age had no place worrying about a phone conversation being interrupted by his parents.

The June evening was mild, and he sat on the back porch, overlooking a hayfield that would be ready for cutting in another week or two. He dialed her number and waited. By the third ring, he assumed it was just going to go to voice mail. Instead, there was a click and her breathless voice said, "Hello?"

"Mel? It's Brett."

A beat of silence. "Hi."

She was breathing hard and he felt compelled to ask, "Is this a bad time?"

"I was out for a run."

He pictured her in short shorts and a T-shirt with her hair in a ponytail and thought she probably looked both adorable and formidable. "I can call back."

"No, it's fine." Her tone said anything but, but he hadn't expected a warm greeting.

"Listen, I just want to talk. About what happened, about what you think happened. I don't like how we left things, you know?"

She'd still been naked and wrapped in a blanket when he'd walked out of her apartment.

"You're the one who left."

"I was offended. And...hurt, to be honest. And unless I was reading things wrong, you were really upset. I'm not sure staying would have helped to clear the air much."

She sighed. "Yeah, you're probably right."

It was a start.

"Maybe we can meet up this weekend. Sunday afternoon or something," he suggested.

"I've got plans on Sunday."

She was not making this easy. And damn it, he hadn't even done anything wrong. He ran his hand over his hair, wondering what to say next, when she spoke again.

"I could stop by on Saturday. I'm driving up to Great Falls for a baby shower Saturday night."

"Saturday afternoon would be fine." He swallowed, inexplicably nervous again. What was it about this woman that got under his skin so easily? "Do you want to meet for coffee again somewhere? Or you could come here. That way you're not locked into a specific time. I'll be here all day."

"You mean come to the Lazy H?"

"Only if you want to."

There was another long pause. "Let me think about it, okay?"

"Of course."

His excited mood deflated. Thinking about it would probably mean waiting a day or two and then cancelling, saying something had come up. But he'd tried. And he did feel better knowing he'd at least reached out to her.

"Mel?"

"What?"

"I swear I didn't know who you were. Please believe me."

"I'll be in touch," she replied, her voice tight. "Bye, Brett."

The connection clicked off in his ear and he frowned, dropping the phone into his lap as he stared out over the fields.

Two dates. It really shouldn't matter what she thought. But it did. More than he cared to admit. If nothing else happened between them, he'd at least convince her that he wasn't guilty of using her.

*

Mel figured she had to be ten kinds of crazy to be visiting the Lazy H after all that had happened. But she was curious. How prosperous was the ranch anyway, that he could afford to beat every offer her cousin had been able to scrounge together? Dustin had offered ten thousand more than Brett's last—her parents had told her that yesterday. And Brett hadn't countered. Maybe he was finally letting it go.

That encouraging thought was the only reason she was driving up the dirt lane leading to Brett's house. Maybe there was some hope for them after all. He'd been the one to call her. He'd invited her here. Maybe, just maybe, he'd reconsidered and was going to tell her to her face.

The Lazy H spread was huge. As Mel drove closer to the house, she saw several barns and outbuildings, long lines of fencing sectioning the rolling hills, and a big, rambling ranch house with a front porch that looked welcoming and a bit worn, in need of a fresh coat of paint. She could tell it was a much bigger operation than her family's. A couple of trucks were parked next to a long building, and she recognized Brett's as one of them.

She pulled up close to the house, next to a silver sedan that looked out of place among all the pickups, and took a breath. He said he'd be home. She'd texted for directions, but that was it. They hadn't actually spoken. Now she was nervous as hell.

The last time she'd seen him, they'd had sex. Mind-numbing, fantastic, amazing sex. And then they'd argued.

What on earth was she going to say?

She cut the engine and took a deep breath, only to have it come out in a whoosh as a woman appeared on the porch. A pregnant woman, she noticed, and one who looked a lot like Brett. Her hair was darker, but the face shape was the same, and so was the mouth. Was this his twin sister, Manda? The one he claimed had set them up?

Maybe this was her chance to go directly to the source for the truth.

Melly pasted on her best meet-the-parents smile and got out of the car. "Hi there," she called, keeping her tone light and pleasant. "I'm Melissa. I'm looking for Brett?"

The woman came down the steps, matching Melly's polite smile with one of her own—but Melly saw that it didn't reach the woman's eyes.

"I'm Manda, Brett's twin sister."

Melly fought back the butterflies in her stomach. "I thought so. You look a lot alike." She would be friendly. It was hardly her first awkward conversation.

"Brett's down in the barn. I can let him know you're here or take you there."

"Whatever's most convenient," Melly replied.

"The barn it is," Manda said, and started to walk across the grass towards the outbuildings.

Melly moved to catch up. "Listen, Manda—"

Manda shrugged. "If you're going to ask, the answer is yes. Yes, I set up his profile and answered your emails. Brett didn't *target* you because of your folks' ranch. He's mighty put out that you thought he'd do something like that."

Wow, talk about not pulling any punches. Forget polite chit chat then. "Did you?" She asked the question bluntly.

"Did I what?" Manda stopped and faced her, her eyebrows pulled together in what appeared to be confusion.

"Did you know?"

Manda stared at her for several seconds, but Melly held the gaze steadily even though her insides were quaking.

"No," Manda said finally. "Melissa, you need to remember there aren't even any last names on the site, so how would I go about doing that anyway?" Her frown deepened. "He could ask the same of you, you know."

"What do you mean?"

"I mean, it's just as plausible that you knew he was trying to buy your folks' place and you hooked up with him to change his mind."

A mix of fury and embarrassment flooded through her. She wanted to ask how dare Manda suggest such a thing but couldn't, because it was exactly what she'd accused Brett of. Her cheeks flamed hot, and she looked away for a moment.

"You're right. I never thought of it that way. It's just...it seemed like too much of a coincidence."

"Hey, I don't know you, so I'm going to go out on a limb here and say I'm guessing that someone, at some point, gave you a reason to be cynical. I know my brother, Melissa. He's a stand-up guy who would never do anything sly or underhanded. He honestly didn't know."

Melly looked back at Manda and sighed. "I want to believe you. I do. That's why I'm here."

"Give him a chance." Manda looked like she was going to say something else, but at that moment Melly's attention was diverted over Manda's shoulder as Brett stepped out of the barn. Her heart gave a solid thump in response to his appearance. He looked good. Better than good, even in a work shirt and jeans and boots. And when he saw her, he halted. The same current that had run between them that first day at the café zinged to life.

Manda followed Melly's gaze and sighed.

"So that's how it is. The two of you are idiots, you know." But there was warmth in the words that had been absent before.

"Sorry?" Melly asked, dragging her gaze away.

"Nothing." Manda started back toward the house. "See you around, Melly."

Brett started walking in her direction, each step strong and deliberate. There was no denying the physical attraction, and between that and Manda's claim of innocence about the situation, Melly was a mess of emotion. She wanted to believe him. And she was terrified it made her weak—and a fool.

"You came," he said, stopping several feet away. "I wasn't sure you would."

"I wasn't either. Not until I actually turned up the lane." She tried a smile. "I met your sister."

"And survived." He grinned at her and a little of the awkwardness dissipated.

"She came to your defense in no uncertain terms," Melly admitted. "And said something that made me think. It's hard for me to believe in coincidences, Brett. It makes me feel naïve and gullible."

"And after your ex, you don't want to feel that way again."

"Yes." She let out a huge breath. He got it. He understood without her having to explain in depth. This was why things had clicked so easily before. And yet there was a little part of her that simply didn't trust it. Or him.

"But you believe me now? That I honestly didn't know of the connection?"

She nodded. "Yes." Their eyes met. "Brett, I think I knew deep down the moment you went out the door. It was just easier than admitting the real truth to myself."

"The real truth?"

"It was easier to blame you than to admit that I reacted as I did because I'm probably not ready to be seeing anyone. I wanted to think I'd moved on. Moved past my anger and my...well, disillusionment is probably as good a word as any."

Brett's smile softened. "Looking in the mirror isn't easy on the best of days. You're here now. That's what matters."

There was a quiet pause as they let everything settle. Then Brett smiled at her and said, "So what do you say? Would you like the nickel tour? We could saddle up a couple of the horses and go for a ride."

It sounded lovely. A warm breeze was ruffling the leaves on the trees and she had a couple of hours to spare. "I haven't gone riding in a while. That sounds fun."

"Perfect. Come with me. I have the perfect horse for you. His name is Charley and he has a soft spot for pretty girls."

Chapter Six

S he'd really come.

Brett glanced beside him, admiring her straight and tall form in the saddle. She'd taken to Charley right away, but then the old gelding had always been a charmer. Brett had watched her hands as they rubbed Charley's neck, heard the soothing sound of her voice as she spoke to the horse while she slipped the bridle over his ears and the bit into his mouth. Despite Brett's best intentions, he hadn't been able to stop himself from comparing her to Sherry. To his recollection, Sherry had never saddled a horse in her life. She'd gone riding now and again when Brett pressed her to do so, but he'd always had to tack the horses so that all she had to do was hop into the saddle.

Melly did it all like she'd been doing it for her whole life...which she probably had.

They rode silently for several minutes. Brett liked that he didn't feel the need to make conversation. There didn't seem to be any awkwardness in the quiet. It wasn't until they were out of sight of the yard and starting an incline that Melly nudged Charlie closer and started speaking.

"This is really beautiful," Melly commented. "But Lazy H is bigger than I expected. You downplayed it a little when we met."

"There are a lot bigger ranches in the area," he replied modestly. "Between my sisters and their spouses, and my mom and dad...well,

I've wanted to strike out on my own for a while now."

"Leave Lazy H behind?"

"Naw." He smiled, took a deep breath of air scented with grass and sunshine. "I still want to be part of Lazy H. Mine will be more of a satellite ranch. I think it'll work really well for everyone involved."

"Won't you miss it here?"

He nodded. "Of course. I grew up here." The horses plodded along, following a path that climbed a rise. "Melly, I understand your attachment to your ranch. I really do. It's why I suggested riding today. I want to show you something."

"You do?"

"Just over this knoll." He pointed with his left hand. "Come on."

He nudged his horse into a trot and heard Charley's hooves following close behind. In no time, he'd reached the crest. The valley spread wide below him, a palette of greens and golden browns of pasture and grain fields, stretching out for miles. A few other ranches could be seen, their buildings dotted in groups in the distance.

Melly came up beside him and reined in, patting Charley on the neck. "Wow. Look at it up here. What a view."

"It's my favorite spot on the ranch," Brett admitted. "Whenever I was troubled or needed to get some perspective, I'd come up here for some peace and quiet. It always made me feel a bit better. Like I was part of something bigger than myself. Like I was connected to something even when I felt alone."

He felt a little silly admitting that to her, but this might be his only chance. She believed he hadn't had an ulterior motive, but that was a far cry from making things right. Starting over. And he wanted to, he discovered. Yeah, he'd been angry at what she'd said. But if he'd been in her shoes, he might have thought the same thing.

He watched her dismount and hold Charley's reins as she walked along the narrow dirt trail, worn from years of travel. Lord, she was beautiful. The way she was looking at the valley right now did something to his heart he hadn't expected. It was healing, he realized. Realizing that someone else could have the same attachment and love for his way of life rather than disparaging it. It was very different having someone care for him because of it rather than despite it.

He also dismounted, and together they walked along the ridge, the warm breeze ruffling his hair and the sun soaking into his face.

How would he feel if someone wanted to take this away from him? Angry. Sad. Helpless.

"Mel?"

She turned her head to look at him. Their steps had grown lazy, and he fought the urge to simply pull her into a hug. There was something in her expression that bothered him. She looked like she appreciated this place, but there was sadness, or maybe resignation too, that dulled her eyes and kept her lips from curving up as he liked.

"I'm sorry," he said quietly.

"For what?" She raised one eyebrow, then broke eye contact and dropped her gaze to the path at her feet.

He reached out and put his hand on her arm. "For circumstances. That your dad isn't up to running the ranch. That you feel like you're going to lose the special places close to your heart."

"I wouldn't if you'd let my cousin buy it instead. It would stay in the family."

He sighed. "Mel, it's not that simple. This is something I've wanted for a long time. I've dreamed of having my own place for as long as I can remember. I know why you're asking it, but you have to realize that for me...you're asking me to give up my dream. It's not an easy thing to do."

"Particularly because we've only been on a couple of dates?" She moved her arm away from his hand. "If you'd never met me..."

"I'd be pretty focused on closing the deal." He let out a breath of frustration. "It's business."

"It's never just business. Not to people like you and me, Brett." Her voice was sharp. "There's a connection that goes from your boots to the earth. You know that."

It burned that she was right. And the one thing he really, really liked about her—that understanding of his way of life—was the one thing that made this whole mess worse.

"After my divorce, I swore if I ever got involved with a woman, it would be with someone who was Sherry's opposite. And now here you are and it's more complicated than ever."

"Would you call us involved?"

"Hell, yes." The question irritated, and he reached out and grabbed Charley's reins, tucking them into his palm alongside the other set. Melly faced him and he saw the defiant set to her mouth, recognized it. Even though he'd known her such a short time, he knew it was the I-must-stand-my-ground expression—but it also meant that she needed to remind herself to hold steady. And he did like a challenge. "Wouldn't you say sleeping together constitutes involved?"

She blushed.

"Mel," he said, his voice slightly lower. He let go of the reins, let them drop to the ground. The horses wouldn't go anywhere, and he wanted both his hands free. He took a step closer to her, saw her pupils widen and her lips drop open just the tiniest bit in surprise, in invitation.

He reached out and gripped her upper arms in his hands. "Doesn't making love mean we're involved?"

Her lips closed. She swallowed, met his gaze and lifted her chin. "Only if it meant something."

Minx. "If it meant nothing, you wouldn't have been so upset afterwards," he replied. And he pulled her closer and kissed her.

She was as sweet as he remembered, sweet and sultry as her mouth opened beneath his. There was no denying the chemistry between them as he let go of one of her arms and moved his hand to her neck, losing it in the thick mass of her soft hair.

She wrapped her arms around his ribs, holding him close, and she made a soft sound in her throat as the kiss took on a life of its own, as wild and free as the waves of grass around them.

He thought briefly about laying her down and making love to her then and there, with the sun warming their skin and the verdant scent of grass and earth surrounding them, but he wasn't prepared. Neither did he want it to be rushed. He wanted to take his time, let them savor each other, maybe on a soft bed with the whole night ahead of them. He gentled the kiss even though his body was raging. "Do you have to go to Great Falls?" he asked hoarsely. "Stay here. Spend the weekend with me."

"With your parents? Really?" She laughed, a breathy, sexy sound that went straight to his groin.

"We'll take off for the night. Get a hotel room. Take a bath with bubbles, make love all night long. It was so good the first time, Mel. I want to try again."

"As enticing as that is, I need to go." She stayed in the circle of his arms though, which he took as a good sign. "It's a shower for a good friend. I can't miss it."

"Well, damn." He trailed his lips down her cheek. "Are you sure?"

"It's tempting, Brett." She turned her head a little and her lips touched his again. This time, the kiss was less heated but no less devastating. Long, deep, lingering.

Melly pulled away, but he got the sense she was doing so reluctantly as she nibbled on her lower lip and looked up at him, her eyes dazed. "There's no denying we do that well, is there?"

"None."

"I wish we didn't. How can I want to be with you so much and be angry with you at the same time?" Her eyes were clouded with confusion. "You're still the man who's going to take away the one thing that means the world to my family."

"And you feel like a traitor?" He kept a firm grip on his irritation. He didn't want to lose his cool like he had back at her apartment. But he did want her to understand that he wasn't trying to destroy anything.

"I feel like a hypocrite, that's for sure." She turned away and reached for Charley's reins. "I can't get past it, Brett. If you'd just leave things be, Dustin could buy it and it'd stay in the family."

"And could the Almighty Dustin manage it was well as I can? Will he build on what's there? How do you know it'll be in better hands than mine?"

She scowled at his cocky words. Damn, he'd spoken without completely thinking it through again, and sounded so arrogant in the process. Still, he wasn't doing a thing wrong, and he was sorry he'd told her his plans. All she'd done was ride his ass about it. Maybe this wasn't worth it after all. He'd enjoyed himself with her, but it was just like he'd told Manda. Women were not worth the headache, no matter how sweet and alluring.

"How do I know?" she asked, her words clipped. "Because he's family."

"And that is a loyal but naïve answer," he replied.

"You know, a few minutes ago, I was hoping we could work something out, but I guess not." She put her hand on the saddle horn and swung herself into the saddle. "I've already been with someone whose arrogance and pride came before our relationship. I won't do that again."

"You think this is arrogance and pride? Which one of us is being arrogant here?" He snatched the reins left trailing on the ground and mounted his horse with a creak of saddle leather. "You've insulted me, judged me, asked me to give up, and the only thing I've expected is, well, some understanding of my position. Newsflash, Mel. You can't stop change from happening. If you're that attached to the place, maybe you should have stuck around and worked it yourself."

He dug his heels into the horse and shot forward, cantering back down the path they'd come. She could find her own way behind him for all he cared. Charley would get her home. His teeth were clenched together and posture ramrod straight as the benevolent sun warmed his back. They had chemistry. He was in no doubt of that. And they had some things in common too. But Brett was starting to realize that there were things missing. Like basic respect, for one.

She'd said she wouldn't repeat past mistakes again. Well, neither would he. The first time he'd chosen wrong, he'd nearly lost Lazy H. He'd be damned if he'd risk this deal, too.

Melly blinked against the stinging in her eyes. Her mouth still hung open from the shock of his last comment. He couldn't have aimed that stab to her heart any better.

She gave Charley a half-hearted nudge and he began to plod his way back down the hill. Melly could see Brett in the distance, his horse taking him farther away with each long, smooth stride.

How many times had she regretted the path she'd taken? She might have stayed home and taken over the ranch as any son would have. But at eighteen, she'd rebelled. She'd wanted to get away. Get her education, be something other than a rancher. In hindsight, she'd taken her home for granted, thinking it would always be there.

At twenty-one, she'd considered it again. But then she'd met James and everything had changed. She liked her job, too. It wasn't that. But there were times she wished she'd done things differently. That she hadn't been so determined to be something or someone she wasn't.

She let Charley walk, plodding his way through the waving grass. Something else was bothering her, too. As much as she liked her cousin Dustin, he was the kind of guy to keep things at the status quo rather than innovate. Under his ownership, the ranch would likely prosper, but it probably wouldn't flourish or live up to its true potential. If Lazy H was anything to go by, Brett could do great things with her family's property. It burned her ass to admit it, but it was true.

She had been arrogant. And prideful. It smarted that he knew it.

When she got back to the barn, Brett was waiting to take Charley. She was surprised at that. She'd figured he'd be nowhere to be seen. But of course, despite his outburst and riding away, Brett had manners. He was a gentleman. Both times when she'd been rude and judgmental, he'd been the first one to reach out.

This time though, his face was a mask of cold politeness as he held Charley's bridle and waited for her to dismount. She hopped down and gave Charley's neck a pat. The earlier silence had been comfortable, but now it was awkward as anything.

"I'd better get going. I still have to drive to Great Falls and get cleaned up before the shower."

"I'll put Charley up. Thanks for coming, Mel."

But his words held little warmth. They were a show of manners, nothing more. It was getting clearer by the second that he'd wanted to bring her around to his way of thinking...and she'd been trying to do the same and they were simply at an impasse.

Any romance was doomed from the start. It was time they faced facts. Some raging libido couldn't make up for all the other problems. They were bound to be on different sides.

"Thanks for showing me around," she replied, suddenly dreading driving away. He wouldn't be calling her again. She knew that as sure as she knew the sky was blue.

She might have said something more, but he was already walking away, leading Charley to the barn. She watched for a few seconds, the way the back pockets of his jeans shifted as he walked away, the straight line of his strong back.

He didn't look back.

Melly sighed and then made her way across the yard to her car. When she drove away, she kept looking in the rear-view mirror to see if he was watching. He wasn't. Today's conversation had completely killed any chance they might have had. He wasn't *the one*. Even though at times she'd thought he could be. It just went to show that ticking all the right boxes didn't mean a damn thing.

Not a damn thing at all.

Chapter Seven

M elly's hand shook as she put down the phone.

It was done then. Brett had outbid Dustin, who'd maxed out his approved financing on his last bid. Before the end of the summer, Brett would take possession of their ranch. Angry tears streaked down her cheeks now that the conversation was over. Not just angry at Brett, but at her parents too. They could have accepted a lower offer and kept it in the family, and they'd chosen not to.

At the bridal shower, her friends had laughingly come up with a solution to all her problems. If she married Brett, she'd get to keep the ranch anyway. So what was the problem? He was good looking and they had chemistry...there were worse things.

But she'd already been in a marriage based on a lie. There was no way she could do that again. And she hardly knew Brett well enough to know if she could ever love him. She wasn't so gullible as to believe that lust and love were the same thing.

She flopped down on her bed and stared at the ceiling. It wasn't fair. If this were a book or a movie, the ranch would be saved and the girl would get the guy and it would all work out. Instead, neither of those things had happened. And she was right back where she started. Alone.

Disgusted, she got up from the bed and went to the kitchen, where her laptop sat on the counter. In moments, she'd booted up and logged on to NotMy1stRodeo.com. Two new hat tips waited for her acknowledgment. Instead, she went to her dashboard and looked at her messages. There was Brett's picture, so handsome and yet a pale likeness to the man she'd met. The photo didn't capture the power of his smile or the heat of his touch. Neither did it touch on the spark of anger in his eyes when he was wronged. And in some ways, she had wronged him. The kicker was she admired him for his perseverance to his goals, the strength of his resolve. She wished her ex-husband had demonstrated more of that strength rather than weakness. And she wished Brett's resolve could have been aimed somewhere other than at her parents' ranch. It was like he said. They both thought they knew what they needed from a partner, but when they got what they wanted, things were more complicated than ever.

Her heart was heavy and there was a lump in her throat as she hit a button that said *delete profile*. When it asked for confirmation, she gave it...and then she was gone. Gone from the site. Enough of online dating for her.

It was time she moved on. From everything and got a fresh start.

Brett hopped out of the truck and smiled at the couple waiting at the bottom of the steps. "Jim. Becky."

"Hello, Brett."

Jim held out a hand and Brett shook it. Over the past month, he'd gotten to know the Carmichaels better, and he liked them. A lot. Having new surveys done and changing the purchase agreement had taken the lawyers some time, but it was all settled now the way they wanted it. Brett was more than satisfied with how it had turned out, and he had Manda to thank once again. It had been her idea to separate the house from the rest of the ranch, enabling Jim and Becky to remain in their home. So Brett had given them the option, knowing that it might be too difficult for them to watch someone else ranch the land.

But they'd accepted, gratefully.

"Coffee's on," Becky said, smiling up at him. "Why don't you come in?"

"Just for a minute," he answered. "I really just came by to pick up the keys to the buildings and barns."

He followed them up the steps while Jim lamented the old days. "Used to be we didn't have to lock our doors around here."

"I know," Brett replied. "For a long time, you just needed a good guard dog. Now it's locks and security cameras."

He sat down at the kitchen table while Becky got coffee from a pot. The house was comfortable and plain, a regular farmhouse much like the one he'd grown up in. The coffee was joined by a plate of cookies and they all sat around the oak table.

"I just wanted to let you know that starting tomorrow, the construction crews will be at the building site." Brett took a sip of coffee. "Hopefully, they won't cause too big of a disturbance."

"It's your place now, Brett. I think you chose a good spot for the house." Jim reached for a cookie.

"Well, it just made sense. I want my own home, and it didn't make sense for you to have to leave if you wanted to stay. It'd be a hard thing to say goodbye to, I think."

"Our daughter certainly thinks so." Jim's face fell a little. "She's very angry with us for selling to you."

"Because you could have sold to Dustin?"

Jim's gaze snapped to Brett's. "You knew about Dustin?"

"I knew more than that, sir." Nerves tangled in his stomach. It wasn't about the deal. They'd agreed to that ages ago. It was Mel. Always Mel. After several weeks, he should be able to leave her behind, but he somehow couldn't.

He put down his cup. "Mel didn't tell you, did she?"

"Melly? What does she have to do with this?"

Wow. Brett had actually been surprised when the Carmichaels had accepted his offer. He figured Mel would have gone to them and pleaded her case, told them everything in an effort to change their minds.

"We met back in May, but I didn't know who she was. She still goes by Walker—"

"Yes, we know," Becky said a little sharply. Brett wasn't sure if that was aimed at him, or due to dislike of the ex.

"It wasn't until we'd seen each other a few times that the pieces came together and she realized it was me who was trying to buy the ranch. She was really mad at me for that, but we'd only been seeing each other briefly and, well..." Brett's face heated. "Truth is, I'm also divorced. This was a big decision, and not one I was willing to let be influenced by a relationship that was so new and uncertain."

"I see."

Brett met Jim's gaze full-on. "Sir, I made it clear to Mel that I didn't know who she was before we went out, and I think she believes that now. But she's still put out that I didn't step aside."

"Is that why you suggested splitting the property?" Becky asked softly.

"Only partly." More than he wanted to admit, if truth be told. He couldn't deny he'd felt better knowing that Mel would still have a place to come home to like she wanted. "I really do want to build my own house," he continued. "But Mel made me think. There is a special connection between a rancher and the land. I know this place means a lot to you, and to her, and so I offered the split if you wanted it. I promise you the operation is in good hands. This way we all get what we want in the end, right?"

There was quiet in the kitchen for a moment. "She doesn't know about the split." Becky's words came out on a sigh. "We were going to tell her, but she decided to go away for a while over her summer break. She's always wanted to go to California and drive up the coast, and I think she chose this summer because she didn't want to be here to see the ranch change hands."

"She probably didn't want to see me either," Brett admitted. "She wasn't very happy with me the last time we saw each other."

"She doesn't know you did this for her, then."

"Did what for me?"

Mel's voice broke through the conversation and the three of them swiveled in their chairs to face her.

"I didn't hear you come in, dear," Becky said, but Mel's gaze was glued to Brett's.

She was so pretty. Her hair was back in a ponytail and her face was tanned, highlighting a few freckles on the bridge of her nose. She was dressed for the heat, in denim shorts and a blue T-shirt and sandals. It made her look about twenty years old.

"Melissa," he said, embarrassed when her full name came out on a croak. She could still make him so nervous.

"Brett."

The word was so cold he was surprised it didn't freeze midair, despite the summer heat.

"Brett's taking possession today," Jim said quietly. "We were just talking things over."

"How long has he given you to pack and get out? Do you know where you're going to live?"

"You might have known these things if you'd stuck around," Becky reminded her, a sharpness to her voice that said she wasn't happy with Melissa's tone.

"It's why I came back."

"No one is going anywhere," Brett announced, impatient. "And I'll explain why, if you'll sit down."

"Another explanation? Each time you give me one of those, Brett, the results are the same. You on our ranch."

"My ranch," he corrected calmly. "Melissa, sit down."

"I don't think—"

"Sit down," he repeated firmly.

With a mutinous set to her lips, she pulled out a chair and sat.

He focused on her. Not on her father or her mother, just her. He wasn't sure he wanted an audience right now, but things needed to be said and he was going to say them. It might be the only time she'd listen.

"I did some thinking after we last saw each other," he began. "And I talked to Manda, too. She knows me best out of all my family. I think it's a twin thing." He smiled a little. Sometimes having a twin was a pain in the ass, but sometimes it was handy. "She knows better than anyone what I went through when my marriage ended. I was left feeling like I was nothing more than a hick with a pitchfork. Sherry had...I don't know, some image of how glamorous life as a rancher would be. Like all the dirty work would be done by the hands and I'd strut around in clean boots and big belt buckles with her on my arm. When she left, in my head I knew she'd simply not been prepared for life on a ranch. I knew that she hadn't really loved the person I was, just the person she wanted me to be. But I think you know as well as I do that the heart can be harder to convince. I felt like less of a man, and it's taken me a long time to want to put myself in that position again."

"Believe me, your manhood has never been an issue."

Brett's face heated a little and he wondered if the blush was noticeable.

Mel's expression had softened a little. "Look, I know I haven't always been fair. It's got a lot more to do with me than it does with you, and in the end it still hurts that the ranch has been sold. Family should come first." Her gaze flitted over her parents. "I would have thought you'd feel the same way. We could have kept it in the family —"

"I like Dustin," Jim spoke up. "He's a good kid. But I'm not sure he's ready to take this on. Both from a work perspective, and from the financial burden. He's got a wife and kids to think about."

Brett leaned over and put his hand over her fingers. "Mel, I always had the best of intentions. I did think about walking away from the deal, you know. But I'd worked for this for so long, and I don't trust easily. How could I logically walk away from it because we'd been out on a few dates?"

"I had started to feel it was more than that," she admitted softly.

"Me too," he agreed, his voice quiet. "But I didn't trust what was between us. It just kept snowballing into a bigger mess. And then, when you walked away, I came up with a compromise."

Her gaze met his, and he could see a little bit of hope there. Just a brief moment, but there was a flash of uncertainty that encouraged him.

"You want to be able to come home," he said, squeezing her fingers. "I understand completely. You want to know that one thing in your life is a constant. I wanted to buy the ranch, but not your life. Not your parents' lives, either. So we had everything re-surveyed and another purchase agreement drawn up. The house and two acres around it still belong to your mom and dad. They can live here as long as they like. And your dad has agreed that if they ever want to sell and move somewhere smaller, you get first crack at the property. I get the second."

Her eyes grew round. "But...where will you live?"

"I'm building my own house south of here. I'm not the enemy, Mel. I promise you, I'm not."

She pulled her hand away and her eyes filled with tears. "I don't know what to say."

"Sweetheart," Becky jumped into the conversation. "We know how hard the last few years have been for you. This wasn't an easy decision for any of us, and we never wanted you to feel like you were, well, displaced. No matter where we are, you can still come home, okay?"

Mel nodded. "I'm still sad. I hate that things have to change."

Brett laughed a little, but it was thick with emotion. "Oh, I know. But sometimes change can be a good thing. Sometimes a person can resist it all they want, and then they get a boot in their ass and end up going for coffee."

Jim and Becky looked confused, but he knew Mel understood, and her lower lip wobbled just a bit. "You should hate me for being such a spoiled brat," she murmured, looking down at her lap.

"Not spoiled. Just scared. And I could never hate you."

The kitchen was silent. He wished they were alone, but he was also glad somehow that the four of them had sat in a room together and talked. Still, there were things he wanted to say without an audience. Things that had little to do with the ranch.

"Mel, let's take a walk."

Mel looked up at him then, and the old chemistry was there, simmering behind her eyes, heavy in the air between them.

Maybe what was between them couldn't be fixed.

But he'd like to have a chance to try. And if it was really over, they could leave it in a better place, without anger and resentment.

Chapter Eight

M elly didn't know what to say. She'd agreed to take a walk, partly because she wanted to hear what he had to say and partly because she really needed a few minutes to get her head in the right space.

The past month, as she and Leanne had traveled the coast, she'd done a lot of thinking. She'd thought about the ranch, about her family, about Brett, and about letting go. She'd come to terms with it for herself, but the idea of her parents leaving the place they'd lived for over thirty years broke her heart. They'd invested so much time and energy and love into the place to just up and leave.

Walking in and seeing Brett sitting at the kitchen table? Her reaction had been so instantaneous, so unexpected that she'd immediately thrown up barriers in the form of hostility. But it wasn't her anger at Brett that had resurfaced. She might have been able to deal with that. It was something else. It was attraction and longing that had slammed into her like a freight train, stealing her breath. After everything, he still had the power to turn her to mush—and all without saying a word.

Finding out he'd made provisions for her parents to stay meant more than she could say. But she had to try. She already owed him an apology. Knowing he'd taken this step simply blew her mind.

Melly knew where she needed to take him. They followed a path behind the house, through the grove of trees to a meadow, and then through more woods until they came to a narrow creek burbling over the rocks and stones.

"It's peaceful in here," Brett commented, letting out a big breath. "I've seen the whole ranch, but I never knew this was here."

"I kept it a secret," she said softly, picking her way down over the bank to the water. There was a spot part way down where the dirt had eroded away from a thick tree root, and it formed a natural seat about four feet wide. Melly eased herself into it and patted the hard earth beside her. "Come sit on my sofa," she invited.

He did, stretching out his long legs. The air was cool in the shade of the trees and the sound of the trickling water was soothing.

"You know your big view back at the Lazy H? This is that place for me." She turned her head and looked at his profile. "I used to come here to ease my tension and stress. It was a busy spot during my teenage years."

He chuckled, the sound low and warm.

"Brett, I'm sorry. What you're doing for my parents...well, I'm not sure Dustin would have done the same." It pained her to admit it, but it was true. Dustin had a family. He would have moved into the house and not thought twice about it. Which would have been his right. Maybe that was what made Brett's compromise that much more amazing.

"It was Manda's idea," he replied, staring at the stream. "Turns out she has some good ones now and again."

"That's generous of you to say. I mean, our first few dates were good up until...well, you know. Until it all blew up. I did a lot of thinking this summer, and I realized my whole perspective was clouded by fear and emotion. It was unfair of me to blame you for everything, or to expect you to change your plans. It had far more to do with feelings I hadn't dealt with yet."

"About James."

"Yeah." She sighed. "I thought I had, but having feelings for someone again, and then finding out you were the one trying to buy the ranch...I thought it was you I didn't trust. Turns out it was my own judgment."

He turned a little, though the seat afforded minimal room. His knee bumped against hers as he looked into her eyes. "You weren't the only one who was stubborn. I considered withdrawing my offer. The fact that it even crossed my mind scared the hell out of me. I felt like you wanted me to change who I was, and I'd already had to do that before, only it failed miserably. Maybe neither of us was ready to enter the dating game again."

Did that mean he wasn't interested now? Not that she deserved another chance after all she'd said.

"The thing is..." Her tongue felt thick in her mouth as she fumbled around for words. "The whole time I was gone, I couldn't stop thinking about you. I thought I'd go away and shake this whole thing off, come back, make a fresh start. Instead, I found you at my parents' kitchen table and everything came rushing back and..." She looked away, embarrassed. "Well."

"What are you saying?" he asked.

She took a deep breath. "Not that I'd deserve it, but I'd like to give us another chance."

That little sideways smile teased his lips. She'd missed that.

"Like go out on a date?"

"Maybe." She looked into his eyes, found warmth and invitation there. "Maybe just take things one day at a time and see where it goes."

He lifted his hand and placed it on the side of her cheek. "You keep saying you don't deserve a second chance. But, Mel, one of the things I did after you left was try to put myself in your shoes. I get it. All of our actions are colored by our past experiences." He smiled, bigger now. "Hey, just because you were wrong about me doesn't mean I don't understand where you were coming from."

She rolled her eyes, amazed that they were actually teasing about this. "I see your ego didn't suffer any permanent damage." She put her hand over his. "Aw, hell, you have to know I'm kidding. You probably have the least ego of anyone I've ever met."

He moved his thumb, rubbing against the tender skin of her cheek, the teasing expression gone from his face. Just tenderness remained, and her heart did a crazy weird thump thing. The sun created dappled shadows around them, the birds in the trees and the rushing stream their background music. And when Brett leaned forward and kissed her this time, she met him halfway, curling her hand around his neck and drawing him closer.

This kiss was different, Melly realized. Better. One hundred times better. There was still sweetness and passion, but now there was something more. Trust. Acceptance. Possibility. All the things she'd wanted and had been searching for.

And when he pulled her into his embrace and wrapped his arms around her, she figured that maybe she'd been right after all. Maybe there really was nothing like a cowboy.

Chapter Nine

The leaves on the poplars and birches were like millions of gold coins, glowing against the blue sky and creating a gilded carpet on the forest floor.

Brett held Mel's cold hand in his as they ambled through the grove, something they often did on Sunday afternoons when she came out to the ranch. Her favorite spot had now become his, too. They often sat on the creek bank and cuddled together, isolated from the outside world. The last time they'd come out here, they'd made love under the canopy of the trees. It had been the first time since they'd decided to start over. For Brett, it had been something particularly precious. It hadn't been the rushed and fevered joining that they'd experienced at the beginning of their relationship. It had been slow and profound. It had stirred something inside him that he welcomed and yet scared him too. He'd fallen in love with her, heart and soul.

"What are you thinking?" Mel asked, nudging his shoulder as they walked. "You're awfully quiet."

"I was thinking about the last time we walked out here," he replied, squeezing her hand.

"Oh, right." She looked up at him and her eyes twinkled at him. "Listen, cowboy, it's getting a little chilly to be sneaking off to have sex in the great outdoors."

"I can think of ways to keep you warm."

"I just bet you can."

He could hear the trickle of the creek ahead, but he slowed his steps, nervous but in a good sort of way. Today was the right time. He wanted to take things to the next step.

So he tugged on her hand, pulling her off the dirt path. The light in her eyes told him that sneaking kisses would be a welcome pastime, so he indulged her by pressing her against a smooth birch trunk and tasting her lips, slowly and thoroughly. As always, her gentle touch made his body spring to life, and before long they were both breathless.

"You're very good at that," Mel whispered, snuggling close against his jacket. "I missed you this week."

"I missed you too." He'd rented a room with a kitchenette at a local motel while the house was being built, and it was damned lonely at night. "Our phone calls just aren't the same as seeing you in person."

"Hey, I showed you how to chat on your laptop."

"Didn't the dating site thing convince you I'm a techno-idiot?"

She laughed. "Maybe you just need to be properly motivated. I'll have to make the view...interesting."

"Tease."

But he loved it. Ever since they'd cleared the air, she'd been so open, so amazing. It wasn't perfect; nothing ever was, and they both knew it. It was, however, a real revelation to be so compatible with someone. They liked and appreciated so many of the same things. She embraced his way of life because she'd lived it and loved it herself, and he'd never experienced that sort of acceptance before. In return, he loved that she preferred these afternoon walks to other more sophisticated activities, where he felt out of place. He was learning that as a teacher she was big on organization, and he was more of a go-with-the-flow kind of guy. But Brett figured that just balanced them out a bit and kept things from being boring.

"Mel?"

"Yes?" She'd stuck her hands in his jacket pockets and was grinning up at him cheekily.

"I love you."

The smile slid from her face, replaced by a look of surprise and what he hoped was wonderment. "Brett," she whispered. "I...wow." Her dark eyes were wide and luminous as she looked up at him. "You...when did this happen? How?"

It wasn't quite the response he was hoping for, but he pressed on anyway. "It snuck up on me, I guess. But last weekend, I knew. When we were together it was...different. Suddenly, it wasn't just me and you anymore, but us."

He cradled her face in his hands. "I don't know how to explain it, other than to say that when I was inside you, something clicked. Fell into place. Like turning on a light in a dark room, you know? It had been coming for a while, but that was the moment that I knew without a doubt that I was in love with you."

She swallowed and her eyes glistened with emotion. "I love you too."

He let out a breath. "Thank God."

Their soft laughter floated away on the air. "When did you know?" he asked.

She stood on tiptoe and kissed his cheek. "So remember the Friday night I showed up and you had the bouquet of daisies that you'd picked? That was the clincher for me. No one has ever picked me flowers before. I remember thinking that this was the sort of man I should have been with all along. If I'd had any hesitation, it was gone after that moment."

"And you didn't say anything?" He'd been tormenting himself all week and she'd already been there?

"I didn't want to be the one to say it first," she admitted, blinking, her lips curving in a sweet smile. "Besides, I thought all you cowboys liked to take the initiative."

He tilted her chin, gazed into her eyes. "Not about everything, minx."

"Hey, guess what?"

"What?"

"I love you."

He couldn't stop smiling. Manda was near impossible these days, crowing about her success as a matchmaker, but he let her because he was happy. For the first time in as long as he could remember, he was perfectly content. He was working his own place, had a woman he loved, and the future was looking at lot brighter than it had a few short months ago.

"I can't wait for the house to be finished," he said, sliding his hands down to her shoulders. "When it is, I'm going to carry you up to the bedroom and make love to you all weekend."

"Mmm. Sounds lovely. Any ETA on that?"

"Contractor says three, maybe four weeks."

"That's a long time."

"Tell me about it."

They started walking back towards the path, their boots making shushing sounds in the leaves.

"Mel?"

"Yes?"

He took a breath and said the other thing that had been on his mind for a while now. "I wish you didn't live so far away."

She laughed. "It's only an hour."

"I know. I miss you during the week, that's all. I know that you have work and then prep and marking and all."

This time she was the one to tug on his hand, halting their progress. "Well, I've been doing some thinking about that myself."

"You have?"

She nodded. Her cheeks were pink from the autumn air, and he was certain that even without any makeup she was the most beautiful woman he'd ever met. Lord, was he getting sappy or what?

"I was thinking about looking for a teaching position a little closer for next year. I mean, I don't want to assume anything, but...well, I'd be closer to my mom and dad. And as far as you and me..."

She touched a finger to his nose. "I'm done with sabotaging the best thing to happen to me by letting doubts creep in. I love you. You love me. And today that's enough. It doesn't get any better than that."

But oh, she was wrong, Brett thought. His heart was full as he gazed into her eyes and caught a fleeting glimpse of forever.

"It gets better all right," he promised. "You just wait and see."

Links

F ind your next great Donna Alward story at www.donnaalward.com! And don't forget to follow Donna on Bookbub, for new releases and special deals announcements! Want more cowboy romance from Donna? Check out THE COWBOY COLLECTION!

About The Author

While bestselling author Donna Alward was busy studying Austen, Eliot and Shakespeare, she was also losing herself in the breathtaking stories created by romance novelists like LaVyrle Spencer and Judith McNaught. Several years after completing her degree she decided to write a romance of her own and it was true love! Five years and ten manuscripts later she sold her first book and launched a new career. While her heartwarming stories of love, hope, and homecoming have been translated into several languages, hit bestseller lists and won awards, her very favorite thing is when she hears from happy readers.

Donna lives on Canada's east coast. When she's not writing she enjoys reading (of course!), knitting, gardening, cooking...and is a Masterpiece Theater addict. You can visit her on the web at www.DonnaAlward.com and join her mailing list at www.DonnaAlward.com/newsletter .

Made in the USA
Monee, IL
07 December 2021

84180440R00121